Handbook
of
Letter
Writing

Johnson Borges

Diamond Publications

Handbook of Letter Writing
Prof. Johnson Borges

First Edition : August 2010
Reprint : February 2014

ISBN : 978-81-8483-323-2

© **Diamond Publications**

Cover Page :
Sham Bhalekar

Published by :
Diamond Publications
264/3 Shaniwar Peth, 302 Anugrah Apartment
Near Omkareshwar Temple, Pune - 411 030
☎ 020-24452387, 24466642

info@diamondbookspune.com
www.diamondbookspune.com

Sale Distributor :
Diamond Book Depot
661 Narayan Peth
Appa Balwant Chowk
Pune 411 030
Tel. - 24480677, 66020282

Contents

PREFACE

You already know how important it is to speak good English in todays global environment. Writing just like speaking is communication. In our letters and e-mails we need to express many things like authority, gratitude, dissatisfaction etc. Expressing ourselves well and with the correct level of formality is an important skill.

The art of writing a letter takes practice, knowledge about proper form and the ability to put into the words, the thoughts and feelings, which are associated with the letter. Learning to write a letter can be difficult, as there are multiple types of letters which can be written. To avoid the time that it may take to learn to write each one of the letters, if you are able to learn to write a basic letter, that will help you create letters for a variety of occasions.

HANDBOOK OF LETTER WRITING has been designed and created keeping constantly in view the above facts. It describes effectively the various strategies to be adopted for better results through correspondence.

The letters in this book reflect a characteristic communication style: simple, direct and together with the modern conveniences of the personal computers, e-mail and the internet, provide you with both a guide to good letter writing and a simple way to automate your correspondence.

350 letters covered in this book provide a good sweep of various forms of personal, business, commercial, secretarial, insurance and banking letters, which can serve as a sound base to emulate and practise. The book describes effectively the various strategies to be adopted for better results through correspondence. A number of model letters have been given to help you draft your own letters suited to the occasion, time and opportunity in your correspondence. I am sure the patient perusal

and study of the book will help you a lot in progressing rapidly on the express way of correspondence towards phenomenal achievements and accomplishments. This book is a valuable, practical, comprehensive and modern guide for all of you who are involved in, and are concerned with correspondence.

I register my sincere thanks to Shri. Dattatray Pashte of Diamond Publications. I am also grateful to K. V. Shigavan of Aksharwel along with his staff.

I hope readers will appreciate this book. Any comments or suggestions for the further development of the book would be most welcome. I can be reached at diamondpublications@vsnl.net

– Johnson Borges

Introduction

Letter writing is not just an art but a necessity in today's world of communication revolution. Though the cyber age has affected the art of letter writing, it has opened new avenues as well. E-mail, is an example. In todays revolutionary world, the formats of letter writing have undergone changes as well. Though this book we have tried to keep you abreast of the latest trends in letter writing.

Classification

Letters are of different kinds. They are broadly classified as follows.

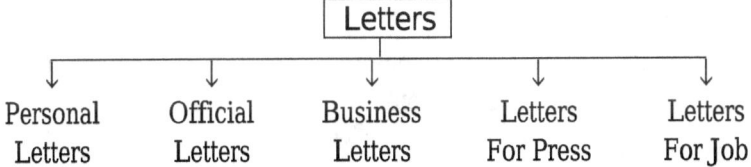

Basic Principles of Letter Writing

(A) Stationary :

The quality of stationary is important. It is the physical appearance of the letter that creates the first impression, and on many occasion the first impression is also the last impression. The reader forms his opinion about you and your business based on the physical aspects of your letter. Hence, it is significant that your letter looks inviting and attractive.

(B) Typing :

Business letters should remain typewriter and grammatical and spelling error free. These types of letters should be legible and professional and there fore typing the letter is one of the most effective ways to ensure that the letter demonstrates a professional appearance thought the entire course of the letter, there by creating a positive impression on the recipient of the letter.

Never type on both the sides of sheet or letter head. Spacing is also important in typing. When the letter is short, it may be typed in double space with triple spaces between paragraphs, paragraphs should present on even and pleasant appearance. They should terminate at logical points. The part of the letter should be typed at their proper places with proper spacing and margins to create harmony, uniformity and balance.

(C) Tone :

While writing a letter one should be natural and relaxed. Always write letter with a positive outlook and frame of mind. Be always courteous and polite even when writing an unpleasant letter. While writing a business letter you must always keep your aim in mind. The tone of your letter should always be pleasant and appealing so that you can convey the message across in order to elicit desired response.

(D) Approach :

Your letter should have "You-approach" in it. It should read as if you are conversing with the recipient.

(E) Brief and Friendly :

As brevity is the soul of wit, use minimum possible words. The more economic you are with your words, the more delightful your letter become. But brevity never means incompleteness.

(F) Planning :

Jot down the main points and then elaborate them logically while writing the letters. You have to be logical, complete and concise to convey your message to the reader.

(G) Simple and Natural :

Short simple sentences and short logical paragraphs make your letter easy and inviting. Use a fresh paragraph for every fresh thought and idea. Develop your idea into message using simple, short and intelligible sentences.

(H) Punctuation :

Make use of punctuation marks and pauses correctly and imaginatively. Punctuation is a means to make writing more easy, intelligible and functional. It is for better to under-punctuate than to over-punctuate.

(I) Grammar :

A misspelled word may create a lot of confusion and misunderstanding and so you must be particular about your spelling, grammar and usage.

(J) Time :

Your letters should reach the recipients when they are most likely to give their most undivided attention.

Time is a most precious commodity and businessman should always use it judiciously and promptly in sending out his letters to customers.

(K) Styles :

Indented style is no more popular though it gives a business letter a balanced and poetical appearance.

The blocked style is preferred because it is more functional, practical, time and labour saving and there fore economical.

Informal Letters

Informal letters are written to people who are close to us or known very well to us. They include letters to parents, brothers and sisters and other relatives.

Such letters are termed informal because the style and format to be followed are casual. You write to such people as if you were conversing with them.

The Form of Personal / Informal Letters

Personal letters, also known as friendly letter and social notes normally have five parts.

(1) Heading :

This includes the address of the person writing the letter, line by line, with the last line being the date. The heading informs the reader where you wrote the letter, and when.

The commas and full stops at the end of the lines are to be omitted.

The date can be written in following ways. 10th July 2009, July 10, 2009.

Example :

> C-1/117, M. G. Road
> Camp, Pune - 411001
> 20th August, 2010

(2) Greeting or Salutation :

The form of greeting will depend upon the relation in which you stand to the person to whom you are writing.

The members of your family, for example, it will be my dear mother, Dear uncle, etc.

To friends, It will be

Dear Anand, Dear Ravi, etc.

Please note that in above examples the use of the term Dear is purely formal, and is a more polite expression, not necessarily implying any special affection.

(3) The Communication or Body of the letter :

Also known as the main text. This includes the message you want to write. The style in which it is written will depend upon the kind of letter you wish to write. The style of a letter to an intimate friend will be very different from that of a purely business letter or an official communication.

Normally in a friendly letter the beginning of paragraphs is indented. If not indented, be sure to skip a space between paragraphs. Skip a line after the greeting and before the close.

(4) Complimentary Close :

The complimentary close should agree with the salutation. It is a formal and polite way to end your letter. The following subscriptions can be used in letters to relatives and close friends :

→ Your affectionately

→ Yours affectionate son / daughter.

→ Yours loving son or brother / sister or friend

→ Yours very sincerely (to friends)

You can also write -

With love and good wishes from your affectionate friend
Rahul Kumar.

While concluding letters to friends and acquaintances whom you addressed as 'Shri' you should use the word 'sincerely' or 'very sincerely', which may be preceded by 'with kind regards.'

As caution, it must be mentioned that sincerely should not be used in letters beginning with the formal 'Dear sir' after which the formal subscription is faithfully or truly.

(5) Signature line :

Type your name. The handwritten signature goes above this line and below the close. The signature line and the handwritten signature are indented to the same column as the close. If the letter is quite informal, you may omit the signature line as long as you sign the latter. In letters to strangers, the signature should be clearly written, so that the reader may know whom to address in reply.

A woman should prefix to the name miss, mrs, kumari or smt in brackets. Ms. can be used by a woman who does not wish to be called miss or mrs.

Postscript - If your letter contains a postscript, begin in with P.S. and end it with your initials. Skip a line after the signature line to begin the postscript.

Example : P. S : I shall try to meet you on sunday.

Yours affectionately,

(Mrs.) Neeta Pandey

Business or Formal Letters

Formal letters are addressed to officials, authorities, would be employers, businessmen, newspaper editors and the like.

Such letters require specific wording and a very definite format.

Form of a Business Letter

A well made up business letter consist of the following parts.

(1) Heading :

In business correspondence almost always letterheads are used. A letterhead generally consist of the company or firm's name postal address, the nature of business and contact numbers comprising telephone, telex, fax and E-mail address.

Reference – Sometimes letterheads may have 'Ref'. Printed on them. This Reference is typed two spaces below the letterhead.

Example :
Ref. NBT/192/PBS

(2) Date :

The date is typed in full in order day - month - year two spaces below the reference.

Example :

Ref. BHU/LT/203

10th August 2009

(3) Inside Address :

The inside address also appears on the envelope. The name and address of the recipient are typed. It should be typed three spaces or more below the date or Ref.

Example :

Mr. Rahul Sen
1023, East street
Camp, Pune - 411001

Sometimes there are special marking in a letter comprising

Attention Line and confidential mark. In case the letter is confidential, it is typed just one space above the inside address in upper case.

Example :

> CONFIDENTIAL
>
> Mr. Arvind Kumar
> Sales Manager
> Bhakti Industries
> 303, Ramgopal Industrial Estate
> Dr. R. P. Road, Mulund (W)
> Mumbai - 400080

Attention line is used when you want your letter to be handled by a particular person. It should be in the upper case or underlined. It should be typed one space below the inside address or above it.

Example :

> Vishv Vijay Publisher
> M-12, connought circus
> New Delhi - 110001
>
> ATTENTION : MR. ROHIT RAI

OR

> For The Attention of Mr. Rajiv Khanna
>
> V - Guard Industries Ltd.
> 44/1037 L.F.C. Road
> Kaloor, Kochi
> Kerla - 682017

(4) Salutation :

Also called greeting. The Salutation in a business letter is always formal. It normally begins with the word 'Dear' and always includes the person's last name or sir, sirs, madam.

Examples

> Dear Mr. Joshi,
> Dear sir/madam,
> Dear sirs,
> Gentlemen,

The salutation is typed two spaces below the inside address or the attention line, and then two spaces below follows the body or text of the letter. But sometimes there is a subject line before the text of the letter. Subject lines inclusion marks courtesy to the recipient. It also helps the recipient to know at once the subject of the letter. It is typed two spaces below the salutation.

Examples :

Sub : Supply of Goods on Credit

Sub : Appointment of Accountant

Sub : Excess Amount Paid

(5) Body or text of the Letter

In business letters the colloquial expressions should not be used. There should be a definite order and it should deal with one subject and unnecessary details should be avoided. The first paragraph should be brief and introductory. In it you are required to introduce the subject of your letter and give reference of previous correspondence if any.

The first paragraph should begin with an attractive sentence in order.

- to arouse the reader's interest.
- to make reference to previous correspondence.
- to say why you are writing to the recipient.

A few examples of opening lines are given below.

(1) With reference to your letter of 8 May, I ....

(2) I am writing to enquire about ....

(3) After having seen your advertisement in .... I would like ....

(4) After having received your address from ...., I ....

(5) I received your address from .... and would like ....

(6) We/I recently wrote to you about ....

(7) Thank you for your letter of 5 July ....

(8) Thank you for your letter regarding ....

(9) In reply to your letter of 10 June ....

(10) Following the visit of your sales managers ....

Closing-Text

Never close your letter with expressions like 'Thanking you', 'Looking forward to your reply', or 'Hoping to hear from you'

The closing line of the text of a business letter should be effective in order -

- to make a reference to a future event
- to repeat an apology
- to offer help

A few examples of effective closing lines are given below -

(1) If you require any further information, feel free to contact me.

(2) I look forward to your reply.

(3) I look forward to hearing from you.

(4) I look forward to seeing you.

(5) Please advise as necessary.

(6) We look forward to a successful working relationship in the future.

(7) Should you need any further information, please do not hesitate to contact me.

(8) Once again, I apologies for any inconvenience.

(9) We hope that we may continue to rely on your valued custom.

(10) I would appreciate your immediate attention to this matter.

(6) Complimentary Close :

It is a formal and polite way to end, your business letter. For this 'yours faithfully', 'yours truly', 'Truly yours' are accepted standard forms.

(7) Signature :

The complimentary close or subscription is followed by signature of the writer or the concerned official. It should be signed in ink and by hand. The use of rubber-stamp signature should be avoided. Below the signature the signer's name and title should be typed. The name and title are typed 4-5 spaces below the complimentary close. Sometimes the name of the firm or company is also typed immediately after the complimentary close.

Examples :

Yours Faithfully Signature Ravi Kumar Manager

Your Faithfully Signature Ram Goyal For Sun Enterprises

(8) Reference Initials :

One space below the signature may be typed Reference Initials. It consist of signer's initials in upper case followed by an oblique and then by typist's lower case initial. This serves as a reminder who prepared and typed the letter.

Example

Your Faithfully Ram Kumar Manager RK/MPS

(9) Enclosures :

Just below the reference initials is typed the Enclosure reminder followed by the number of enclosed items.

Example

Encl. : 5

(10) Copies to be Circulated Notation :

This is a courtesy like Enclosure to let the recipient know to which third party the copy of the letter has been sent. It is indicated by typing 'CC' followed by the name of the recipient of the copy of the letter.

Example :

Encl. : 4 CC Mr. Kartik Sahani, Sales Manager

(11) Envelope :

The envelope should always match the letter in quality, size and colour. The address should be typed in single space about half way down and leaving proper space margin to the left.

□ □

Useful Phrases For Letter Writing

(A) Phrases for Personal and Social Correspondence

Openings :

The standard opening for personal correspondence is Dear but variations include :

My dear....

My dearest....

Darling....

Useful Phrases :

Thank you for your letter [inviting, offering, confirming]

I am very grateful to you for [letting me know, offering, writing]

It was so kind of you to [write, invite, send]

Many thanks for [sending, inviting, enclosing]

I am writing to tell you that

I am delighted to announce that

I was delighted to hear that

I am sorry to inform you that

I was so sorry to hear that

Closures : For acquaintances and formal situations

Best wishes

With best wishes

Kindest regards

Closures : Affectionate variations for close friends and family

All my love

All the best

Love
Lots of love
Much love
With love
Love from us both
See you soon
Once again many thanks
I look forward to seeing you soon
With love and best wishes
With love to you all
Do give my kindest regards to....

(B) Phrases for Letters about Employment

Openings :

The standard opening for formal correspondence is Dear

Dear Sir	Dear Mr
Dear Madam	Dear Mrs
Dear Sir or Madam	Dear Ms
Dear Sirs	

Useful Phrases :

I am writing in response to your advertisement in [publication]
I am writing to apply for the post of
I should be pleased to attend an interview
Thank you for your letter of [date] offering me the post of
I am delighted to accept the position of [job title]
I look forward to starting work with you

Closures :

Thank you for considering this application
I should be pleased to attend an interview
Please do not hesitate to contact me on the above number if you should require further information
I look forward to hearing from you

If you know the name of the person use :

Yours sincerely

If you don't know the name of the person use :

Yours faithfully

(C) Phrases for Business Letters

Openings :

The standard opening for formal correspondence is Dear

Dear Sir	Dear Mr.
Dear Madam	Dear Mrs.
Dear Sir or Madam	Dear Ms.
Dear Sirs	

Useful Phrases :

Thank you for your letter of [date] concerning

Thank you for sending me a [catalogue, quotation]

Thank you for your enquiry of [date]

I refer to your letter of [date] concerning

I apologise for the delay in replying

As stated in your letter/fax of [date]

I wish to draw your attention to the

I wish to inform you that

Further to our Telephone conversation of [date]

I am writing to confirm our telephone conversation of [date]

I would be grateful if you could forward me a [price list, catalogue]

I am contacting you regarding

I am writing to complain

I am writing to inform you that

I am writing to express my dissatisfaction with

Please note that

Please find enclosed

Closures :

> I look forward to hearing from you
> I look forward to hearing your response
> I would be most grateful if you would look into this matter as soon as possible
> Please let me know as soon as possible what action you propose to take
> I trust that you will give this matter your urgent attention
> I hope you can settle this matter to my satisfaction
> Please do not hesitate to contact me should you require further information
> Please contact me if you require further details
>
> If you know the person's name use:
> Yours sincerely
>
> If you don't know the person's name use:
> Yours faithfully

□ □

Useful Tips For Letter Writing

Letters of Greetings

- Here's wishing you a very happy and most exciting Christmas.
- Here's wishing you a happy birthday and many happy returns.
- Please accept my heartiest greetings on the occasion of Diwali.
- I would like to offer you my best/warmest wishes on the occasion of your wedding anniversary.
- May everyday of your future be as delightful and auspicious as this day.
- I'm very much disappointed because I shall not be with you on the occasion.
- What a pity I shall miss being with you on this Christmas.
- I'd love to be with you but
- I wish I could be with you
- I'd love to be with you
- Do enjoy yourself
- Do have a nice time
- With best wishes and warm regards.

Letters of congratulation

- It floods my heart with joy to learn about your .....
- I was on cloud 9 when I read/heard about ....
- It was great to hear about .... Congratulations.
- It was thrilled to hear/read .... Congratulations.
- Let me congratulate you ....
- Allow me to offer my heartiest congratulations ....

- I am sure you are on your way to wining greater glory.
- May God bless all your future endeavours.
- Do you plan to celebrate this occasion
- So what are your plans now? I think you should ....
- So when is the party coming.
- Congratulations again and may God bless you.
- If feels good to have a friend of your standing. Keep it up.

Condolence Letters

- It was with deep sorrow that I heard this morning of your terrible loss....
- It was with much distress I learnt about ....
- Please accept my heartfelt sympathies on the loss of your beloved father.
- I was extremely/dreadfully sorry to hear about the loss of your beloved ....
- I was shocked to learn about the untimely demise of your ....
- I express my heartfelt sympathies in the grief you must be feeling.
- He was such a lovable man. Indeed his passing away is an irreparable loss to you and to all of us.
- May God grant his soul eternal rest and give you enough courage to withstand this shock.

Letters of Sympathy

- I am/was so sorry to hear that ....
- I am/was extremely/dreadfully/awfully sorry to hear ....
- I am/was deeply sorry to learn ....
- I am/was most upset ....
- It was with much distress I learnt about ....
- I shall be only too willing to be of any help to you.
- I shall be glad to help you if necessary.
- Please feel free to let me know if I can be of any help.
- Do take care of yourself.
- With best wishes for a speedy recovery.

Letter of Invitation

○ I am throwing a party to celebrate my 21st birthday on 22nd April 2010 at 5p.m. at my residence.

○ I shall be very much pleased if you come with your family to grace this occasion.

○ We should be very pleased if you could ....

○ We should be delighted if you could ....

○ It would be a pleasure to have as one of our esteemed guests.

○ Do honour us with your presence.

○ We are eagerly looking forward to have you with us.

Letters Expressing Regrets

○ Thanks a lot for your invitation to attend ....

○ I was thrilled to receive the invitation for your ....

○ It was very kind of you to remember me on the occasion of your ....

○ Thank you.

○ You must be thinking me very rude for my failure to attend your party yesterday, but let me assure you I just couldn't help.

○ I would have been delighted to be with you but ....

○ I was thrilled to receive your invitation for your .... party and was looking forward to meeting you but owing to ....

○ It was my ardent wish to make it to your party but owing to reasons beyond my control I could not make it.

○ Nevertheless I convey my heartiest good wishes to ....

○ All the same, please accept my hearty congratulations.

○ I honestly regret the disappointment I may have caused you by my absence.

Thanking Letters

○ Thank you very much

○ I wish to express my sincere gratitude for the beautiful birthday gift you send me.

- Thanks a million for your love and cooperation during my illness.
- It was extremely good of you to remember me
- I am immensely grateful to you for ....
- I am extremely obliged to you ....
- I am extremely obliged to you for being a pillar of strength to me during my father's illness.

Ten Useful Tips For Job Application

(1) The job application should have a professional look. The layout of the letter should be pleasing. A standard business-letter format should be used.

(2) The job application must reflect the applicant's confidence in his/her capabilities. However, sounding over-confident or complacent should be avoided. The very important thing is that the tone of the letter should be consistently positive.

(3) While writing job application care should be taken to avoid sounding indifferent, stiff, too reserved. Showing interest and concern is important.

(4) Specific details of the applicant's education, training, experience, reference and skills should be emphasized.

(5) Facts that demonstrate the applicant's skills and capabilities should be stressed.

(6) Care should be taken to use correct numbers, dates, names and references.

(7) The application should be well organised.

(8) Utmost care should be taken to ensure that grammar, usage, vocabulary and punctuation are correct.

(9) Express eagerness to meet the employer or directly ask for an interview.

(10) Try to highlight your strength and describe your capabilities, achievements.

□ □

Example of Letter-head

Fax : 044-23456783
Phones : 22151308 (EPABX)
22161308 (marketing)

E-mail : Marketing @ Kaveri
cement. com
Website : www.kavericement.com

KAVERI CEMENT

Trusted By Engineers

Marina mansion, Vth Floor, 20 Ethiraj Salai Egmore,
Chennai - 600008

Technovision

Creating a wonderful new beginning with home-appliances

D - 103, Verna Electronic City, N.H.17, Goa - 403111
Tel : 0832-3525498, Fax - 0832-3526588
E-mail : technovision @ yahoo. com

Format of Letter

There are several letter formats, but all of them can be subdivided into two basic groups. These two groups are 'Block Format' and 'Indented format'. These days blocked format is preferred because of its many functional advantages. It is more economical and convenient.

(A) Block Format

In 'Block Format' letter (1) All text is aligned to the left margin (2) paragraphs are not indented. In this style straight edge method is adopted in writing the date, inside address etc. Here the lines are flush to the left and there are no punctuation marks at the end of the lines. There is no period after the date as well.

(B) Indented Format

Some people still prefer indented format to block format because it is more appealing, and poetical and imparts dynamic look to your letter.

SAMPLES

(1) Block Format (Friendly Letter)

C - 17, Madhuban
Paud Road, Kothrud
Pune - 411038
10th April 2010

Dear Kunal,

....

....

....

....

....

....

Yours affectionately
Rajat Kohli

(2) Indented Format (Friendly letter)

B-103, Shivganga
508, Narayan peth
Pune-411030
July 10, 2010

Dear Pranav,

....
....
....

....
....
....

....
....
....

With regards
Rahul Das

(3) Block Format (Business Letter)

Everest Equipments
B-11, 2nd Floor
Commercial complex
Ethiraj Salai
Chennai - 600008

Ref :
July 10, 2010

The Manager
State Bank of Mysore
K. G. Road
Bangalore - 560254

Dear Sir,

Sub : ....

....

....

....

....

....

....

....

Yours faithfully
Sd-
(Jay Mohan)
Proprietor

(4) Indented Format (Business Letter)

                                        Everest Equipments,
                                        B-11, 2nd Floor,
                                        Commercial Complex,
                                        Ethiraj Salai,
                                        Chennai - 600008
                                        July 10, 2010

Ref :

The Manager
State Bank of Mysore
K. G. Road
Bangalore - 560254

Dear Sir,

Sub : ....

....
....
....

....
....
....

....

                                        Yours faithfully
                                             Sd-
                                        (Jay Mohan)
                                          Proprietor

Another Example of Business Letter (Block Format)

Digital World
8, Sagar Arcade
F. C. Road
Pune - 411004

Ref : ....

June 15, 2009

CONFIDENTIAL
The Manager
Sys-Tech Computer,
B-15, Vega Center
Shankar shet Road
Swargate, Pune - 411042

ATTENTION :...

Dear Mr......

Sub : ....

Yours faithfully
Sd-
(Rahul Pandey)
Proprietor
RR/JVK
End : 6
CC : Mr. ....

□ □

Curriculum Vitae (CV) and Resume

Curriculum vitae or a resume is an integral part of job application. The term 'curriculum vitae' is more specific to 'bio-data'. It refers to 'a brief objective account of a person's education, qualifications and previous occupations. Unlike bio-data, it does not include a comprehensive section on personal details. CV is more professional than 'bio-data'.

The term 'resume' is more common today. It is a job-specific summary of one's professional background, education and experience.

In short we can state that both bio-data and CV are general, while a 'resume' is specific and audience centered.

Now a days bio-data is outdated with most organisations going in for either a CV or a resume.

Example of CV and Resume are given bellow.

Example OF CV

---

(1) Personal Profile

    1.1 Name   : RAHUL GOVIND SHUKLA

    1.2 Date of birth : 15 March, 1985

    1.3 Address   : 2/A, Trilok Hights, Kalbadevi Road,
                      Mumbai - 400002
                      Phone : 9600231305
                      E-mail : rahul-shukla@hotmail.com

---

(2) Educational Qualifications :

Degree	University/ Institute	Year	Subjects	Division/ grade
B.E. (Civil)	Government College of Engineering, Pune.	2003	-	I
XII	St. Vincent Jr. College Pune	1999	-	I
X	St. Vincent School Pune	1997	-	I

(3) Work Experience

Post	Organisation/ company	Period	
		From	To
Project Engineer	Kaveri Infrastructure, Bengaluru	15/03/2008	Contd
SR. Engineer	Magna Constructions Bengaluru	10/11/2005	14/03/2008
Site Engineer	Magna Constructions Bengaluru	8/8/2003	9/11/2005

(4) Activities

Extra - Curricular Activities

○ Member, Bengaluru Industrialists Forum.

○ Captain, College cricket Team - Feb. 2000 - Oct. 2002

○ Took part in state level cricket Tournaments

○ Stood 4th in Bengaluru Marathon - 2008

Hobbies

○ Chess

○ Adventure Sports

Example of Resume

NIKHIL SANJAY GUPTA
NEETA VILLA, 118, 18th June Road
Panji, GOA - 403001
E-mail : nikhil-gupta@yahoo.com

POSITION SOUGHT	: Project Manager
OBJECTIVE	: To work as a project manager in a premium research Institute, where I will have opportunities to use my experience in Applied Research and Product Development.
EDUCATION	: Manipal Institute of Technology, Manipal B.Tech in Computer Engineering, July 2004.
EXPERIENCE	: Manager (operations), sigma systems, Bengaluru.

○ Liasoning work
○ Execution of MOU
○ Knowledge Management
○ Forming alliances

SPECIAL SKILLS : ○ Excellent communication skill
○ Presentation and Interpersonal skill
○ Competent in speaking French and German

ACTIVITIES AND : ○ Associate Member of Institution of
INTERESTS   Engineer, Kolkata
○ Member, KCCI, Bengaluru
○ Cricket, Football, Lawn Tennis.

ACHIEVEMENTS : MIT Merit Scholarship, 2002

REFERENCES : Prof. Ramkrishna Murthy
Manipal Institute of Technology, Manipal.
Murthyr@rediffmail.com

Text of The Letter

1. Apology to a Friend

Dear Abhishek,

I hope you reached home safely on Monday night. I felt really bad about the whole episode; and I am extremely sorry for having offended you.

I regret the way I treated you. In fact I was very disappointed at losing the finals of the hockey match. It was definitely my mistake that allowed the opponent team to score the deciding goal. However, I still feel that it was not just my lapse which resulted in our loss. Since you solely blamed me for the debacle, I lost my composure altogether as well as my sense of reasoning. The frustration and disappointment overtook me completely. I hope you can understand my mental agony I am suffering from at present. Please, therefore, forgive me and forget my nasty temperament which was a reaction of losing the match. I am really ashamed of my behaviour. I still consider you as my best friend.

Do reply if you have forgiven me. I will be waiting anxiously for your reply.

2. Condolence to Friend Who has Recently Lost His/Her Mother

Dear Mohan,

The news of your dear mother's sad and untimely demise came as a rude shock to all of us. We cannot believe that she is no more with us.

We knew that she was ailing. But we always hoped that she would recover. This is a tragic personal loss to me. She was such a sweet dear lady, always so hospitable and I knew she loved me very much. For you it must be even more terrible. How are all of you coping? The house must feel terribly empty. It is up to you now to give courage to your father and to your little sister.

I pray that her soul rest in peace and as soon as it is possible I shall come to pay you a visit. Until then keep courage. May God give you the strength to bear this tragic loss.

3. To Friend, about Your Daily Routine

My dear Rajeev,

Many Many thanks for your letter describing the village life in your State. I am really impressed about the excellent routine of your life in your village which keeps you healthy, wealthy and wise. It is chiefly because of the disciplined life of the rustic people in our country.

In this letter I would like to tell you something about my daily routine. It is more or less the same for most of the school going children of this region.

I get up at 5.30 in the morning. Then I study for about two hours. At about eight I take bath and have my breakfast. From 8.30 to 9.30 I do my home task. Then I take my meal and leaves for school at ten.

Our school begins at 10.30 and closes at 4.30. We learn three languages and one craft. We have to offer three optional subjects at the +2 stage. We play different games from 4.30 to 5.30 Then we go home.

On reaching home I wash my hands and feet.

Thereafter I watch T.V. for some time before taking my dinner at 8.00. Then I study for about two hours and go to bed at ten.

On sundays and holidays I go to visit my cousins. On some holidays we go to the cinema. Besides this I have to wash and iron my clothes on Sundays. I enjoy reading magazines and novels in the afternoons. This is how I have planned my daily routine which I keep throughout the year.

4. To Friend, Apologizing to Him for Having Failed to Keep an Appointment

My dear Rohan,

Please do not be angry or upset with me. Hear me out first. I am sorry that I could not attend your birthday party yesterday evening. Now let me explain why.

I left home quite early in the afternoon. I was standing at the bus-stop close to my house waiting for a bus. In the meantime, my brother came and told me that our sister who was playing by the roadside was knocked down by a cyclist and was badly hurt. I rushed her to hospital, where she was treated as an out-patient and discharged after two hours. By the time I came home. It was 9 p.m.

This is reason why I could not attend your birthday party.

I am sure you will understand and excuse me. Do write soon.

5. To Uncle, Thanking Him for the Help

Dear Uncle,

Let me first of all say a really big 'Thank you' to you from the bottom of my heart for the help and comfort you provided us during your stay here.

Daddy being abroad, I would never have been able to cope with mother's illness the way you did. You were like an angle in disguise. Had you not been here to help us, mother's illness might have grown worse. You came here intending to spend a few days in rest and relaxation. I am really sorry that it turned out to be such a tense time. You had to do trips to the hospital every day with all of us, taking turns to be with mother.

I have written to Daddy about your wonderful and timely help during this very trying time. You came to us like a Good Samaritan. All of us, including mother, thank you very much for what you have done for us.

6. To Younger Brother, about the Importance of Good Health.

My dear Ravi,

I am very glad to know that you have passed your Intermediate examination in the first division. I most heartily congratulate you on your grand success. God has given the reward of your labour and I wish you even success in your future life.

However, when you came home last time, we were all worried about your poor physique. It seems you have forgotten the common saying "all work and no play makes Jack a dull boy." You are hero in studies but zero in sports. As an elder brother I shall advise you not to neglect your health and be lazy. You must do some exercises and also play any game you are interested in. It will keep you physically fit and mentally alert. It will enhance your concentration in studies and shape your body well. Good health will save you from physical ailments which you will be afflicted with in the absence of health care.

Therefore, pay adequate attention to my advice. Do not keep on neglecting your health.

You should take milk and fruits in your diet. We will increase your daily allowance.

I hope you will pay required, attention to your health. With love and best wishes.

7. To Friend, Informing Him What You Want to Do after Your Final Examination

My dear Rajat,

I hope this letter finds you in the best of your health and equally. We all are the highest of spirits well here.

I have received your letter and noted the contents. I am happy to note that your preparation for the ensuing examination is going on well so very well.

You have asked me what I intend to do after my examination. At present nothing is decided; my whole attention is focussed on my examination. Work at hand is the most important thing in the world. However, I think that the youth of today should do something independently. I wish to become an enterprising man. So I intend to start a modern bakery with the help of some bank loan. In fact, I don't want to take any financial support from my parents at this initial stage. I don't know whether you approve of my plan or not. Any way, please send your unreserved comments on it; I may change to something new. But as you know 'one must not count one's chickens before they are hatched.' I close the topic for the present.

I think your papa and mummy are doing well. Convey them my regards. Love to your younger brother.

With love and good wishes,

8. To Niece, Congratulating Her on Her Success.

My dear Gauri,

I know that I already congratulated you when I phoned this morning, but I want to congratulate you all over again. Three cheers for you!

I just can't believe it. Your winning the first prize at the state level elocution competition! Do you remember how I used to tease you for your lisping last year? Surely, you have really come a long way.

All of us are proud of you. Mummy never stops telling the neighbours and visitors about you, and Daddy is planning to buy you a present. Mohan boasts about you to all his friends at school. We just can't get over this grand achievement of yours.

I shall be coming these holidays to Pune and then I shall congratulate you personally and tell you how proud I am to have a niece like you.

Three cheers, once again!

9. To Father, Informing Him of Your Success in the Examination.

Dear father,

As you know, I had gone out on a historical tour last week. On my return today in the morning. I got the happy new that I have cleared the entrance examination for admission in Indian Institute of Management with flying colours since my All India Rank is 72. I hope that I shall have the choice to join the top-most institute of the country for pursuing my Master of Business Administration Course.

This is really a proud moment of my life and I feel on top of the world. With the degree from IIM Ahmedabad, all my dreams will come true. Now I shall be able to join the corporate world of business as the top rung in the ladder. The credit of my success partly goes to my college teacher heights in my life. But the real credit goes to you and mom for having selected a very good college for me. But for you and the consistent advice of mummy, I would not have been able to find a place and rank as high as I have got. Now I have a bigger challenge and that is to excel in the course. However, I am optimistic that with your blessings and continued support, I shall be able to bring laurels to my parents and to all those of my well-wishers who stood the test of time in assisting me by giving the requisite support at any time I needed it.

Please convey my best regards for mummy and love to Vishal.

10. To Younger Brother, Advising Him to be Serious in His Study.

My dear brother,

I received your letter today in the morning. I am glad to read that you have passed the half-yearly examination with good marks. But you must remember that your High School Examination is drawing near. You must study well and try to secure good marks in the examination.

You must prepare complete syllabus thoroughly well. Don't try to take short-cuts as many students are tempted to do believing that if they are lucky enough, they will get the same questions in the examination papers that they have prepared. Such students often repent in their life. As you know, hard work is the key to success, you must therefore be industrious in your studies. Plan your routine in such a manner that you get maximum benefit without sacrificing your other concerns like light entertainment and health. If you ever face any problem at any stage, feel free to consult me. I shall assist you the maximum I can.

Pay my regards to mummy and papa.

11. To Friend, To Spend Summer Vacation with You.

My dear Anurag,

Thanks for your kind letter. I am quite well here and hope the same for you. I am very glad to note that you have done your papers well.

Your examinations are over now and your college is closing for summer vacation. This is the time to take rest and prepare for the next session. I therefore invite you to spend a part of your summer vacation with us at. Life is very slow and interesting here. You will really enjoy your stay.

I have already discussed about your arrival plans with my father and made plans for sight-seeing. He has promised to hire an air-conditioned cab for a week to enable us to enjoy ourselves.

I hope you will approve of these plans and write to me soon, preferable by the return post.

Hoping for an early reply.

12. Advice to Cousin Brother

Dear Sachin,

Received your letter yesterday. I fully understand your situation. Deciding on a career is one of the most difficult jobs in the world. But remember, the most important thing is to know what your capabilities are and then decide what you want.

As far as I can see, you don't like science, and you are a good speaker. This makes you capable of teaching or being a lawyer.

I think your ability to argue your way out of any situation will stand you in good stand in a courtroom. You also are an avid reader of crime fiction. So, law is not a totally unfamiliar subject for you. Infact, I am surprised the idea didn't already occur to you. Maybe you are wary of the difficulties in becoming a lawyer. I wouldn't let that worry me if I were you. What is important is determination. If you like imparting knowledge, why then, teaching is the line for you.

I'll think about other careers, and then I will write again. Till then keep your chin up, and don't worry, something good will turn up.

Do write soon.

13. To Uncle, Thanking Him for the Birthday Gift He has Sent You.

My dear Uncle,

Thank you so much for the fantastic birthday gift you have sent me. I do not know how you guessed that this was exactly what I wanted!

I have now developed a taste for music and I like playing popular musical instruments. I have recently joined a class for violin lessons and made good progress in it. You have sent me my favourite musical instrument just at a time when I was thinking about getting one.

My friends also liked the gift and they too wondered how you had the idea to choose the right type of gift.

Please convey my regards to dear Aunty and Grandpa.

14. Congratulations on Marriage

Dear Ramesh,

We were must delighted to receive the news of your marriage in Mumbai last Monday. We are sorry that we could not come to attend it as we did not receive the invitation in time.

Bath of us sent you our heartiest congratulations. We also wish both of you a very happy and prosperous married life.

With best wishes.

15. Enquiring about an Accident

Dear Uncle,

We were all much worried and pained to hear that you had met with a car accident while returning from Kolhapur.

Nobody has as yet informed us about the full details and injuries suffered by you. Dear mother is very anxious to know about your welfare. We tried to contact you on your office telephone yesterday but were informed that you are on long leave.

Please inform us about your latest condition because both Papa and Mummy want to visit you to enquire about your health. If we do not receive any letter from you soon, then Mummy and Papa will leave for Pune.

We are anxiously waiting to hear from you by return of post and wish you quick recovery.

With regards,

16. To A Friend, Who is in Hospital

My dear Pravin,

I have just come to know from your younger brother that you are admitted in the hospital for the last seven days. I am so sorry to know about this.

I know that you have been suffering from this ailment for sometime past. It is good that now you are in hospital and proper treatment can be given to you for ending this trouble once for all. I hope you must have felt better in these even days and it will not be long before you are completely cured. I hope that hospitalisation will give you the much needed rest about which you never cared. Kavita is sending you some of your favourite books which you can read to pass you time.

Kavita joins me in wishing you a quick and complete recovery.

With best wishes.

17. An Invitation to a Dinner Party

Dear Rohan,

We are arranging a small dinner party to celebrate our first wedding anniversary on sunday evening i.e. 15 October, 20...

We cordially invite you to this dinner party. We hope that it would be convenient for you to dine with us. We are also inviting some of our close friends and relatives on this occasion.

Dinner will start at 8.30 P.M.

With best wishes,

18. Acceptance to Invitation

Dear Ashok,

Thank you so much for your kind invitation to dinner on Sunday evening.

We shall be very glad to join you for dinner and meet your close friends and relatives.

With best wishes,

19. Invitation to a Picnic Party

Dear Rakhi,

We intend to go to water park near Sinhgad for a picnic on Sunday, the 18th February, 20.... We are going by car and would very much like you to accompany us for this outing.

Please let me know at your earliest if you would be able to join us along with your family members.

Hoping to hear soon from you.

20. Acceptance to Invitation

My dear Geeta,

Thanks for your kind invitation for a picnic at the water park near sinhgad on Sunday the 18th February, 20....

We all accept your invitation with great pleasure and will reach your residence on Sunday the 18th February, 20.... at 7.30 A.M. I hope that all of us will have a good time on that day.

Wishing you all the best.

21. To Yoga Expert, Inviting Him to Inaugurate the Yoga Club

Dear Mr. Desai,

Our school plans to have a Yoga Club. We desire to get it inaugurated on 2nd October 20--. You are renowned in Nagpur for your Yoga skills. It will indeed be an honour if you accept our invitation to inaugurate this club. It would not only be an inspiration for our members, but also an apt occasion for you as a teacher to advise us on one of the greatest sciences this country has even given birth to.

We are aware that you have a busy schedule, but sincerely request you to make it possible. Do let us know through the person who will bring this letter to you. The programme will begin at 8.00 a.m. in our school ground. The whole school will be in attendance.

Thanking you in anticipation,

We remain,

22. Request for Catalogue

Dear Sirs,

Please send us a copy of your latest catalogue and price list and let us know your best terms for wholesale buyers.

23. Reply to Above

Dear Sirs,

We thank you for your letter No. --, dated the -th November 20--, and have pleasure in sending herewith a copy of our latest catalogue and price list.

We need hardly add that we are makers of quality products for the last fifty year and despite every competition, our products stand first in sale.

Our list prices are subject to a trade discount of 20% and an additional commission of 20% will be allowed in case your annual purchase from us exceed Rs. 50,000.

We now await your order, which as usual will receive our most careful consideration and prompt attention.

24. Supply of Articles

Dear Sirs,

We have the pleasure to introduce ourselves as dealers of home-made pickles, jams and jellies. We prepare our products according to the best recipes gathered over years of experience, and we use the best spices, fruits and vinegar in their making.

We enclose a list of our varieties which, we are sure, will immediately catch up your market. We shall offer you 10% trade discount along with 30 days credit facilities.

Assuring you of the best of our attention and cooperation.

25. Enquiry for Steel Furniture

Dear Sirs,

Please send us your lowest quotation for :

1. Storewell Cupboard with four adjustable shelves ....2 pieces.
2. Two Drawer Foolscap size Filing Cabinets deep fitted with automatic lock, ball bearing slides and compressor plates .... 5 pieces.
3. Steel Trays .... 12 pieces.

Quotations should reach by 24th March 20--.

26. Reply to Above

Dear Sirs,

We thank you for your inquiry No. 1647 dated the 13th March and have pleasure in submitting our estimates for supply of your requirements as under :

1. 2 "Storewell" cupboords fitted with our adjustable shelves making five compartments, with steel doors : Rs. 6800/- each.

2. 5 Filing Cabinets, foolscap size, having four drawers, funning smoothly on ball bearing suspensions, each drawer with compressor, label-holder and handle complete with automatic locking device : Rs. 3500/- each.

3. 12 Steel Trays Rs. 150/- each

Prices   : All prices are inclusive of free delivery at Mumbai.

Colour   : Steel Gray or Olive Green as may be required.

Sales Tax   : Will be charged extra @ 10%

Delivery   : Items 1 and 2 in about one month's time. Item 3 in one week's time.

Payment   : Full payment to be made against delivery of goods.

Validity   : Our offer is valid for one month from the date here of.

We enclose herewith our illustrated leaflets on the items offered by us for your information.

All parts of the materials will be subject to thorough antirust chemical and mechanical treatment before being applied a coat of anit-corrosive paint and sprayed under pressure with finest oven-baked enamel.

Awaiting your further valued instructions, and always with pleasure at your service, we remain,

27. Quotations for Wholesale Supplies

Dear Sirs,

We wish to keep your publications in full assortment and in bulk quantities of say 50 to 100 copies of each title. As soon as one or more titles get exhausted we shall go on replacing them, so that we always have full variety of your books.

Needless to say, the books are required for wholesale purchase and hence your most favourable terms are requested.

Thanking you,

28. Reply to Above

Dear Sirs,

We thank you for your letter dated__

We have pleasure in enclosing our current price list together with discount terms as mentioned therein.

We shall be glad to offer additional 10% discount on orders over Rs. 15000/-.

The goods are supplied in cardboard cartons covered with gunny packing and are sent F.O.R. destination railway station.

The documents will be sent through your bankers.

We hope you will find the above terms acceptable and shall send us your first bulk order at an early date which will receive our most careful consideration and prompt attention.

Meanwhile we thank you and assure you of our best co-operation always.

29. Quotation for Crockery

Dear Sirs,

Please send us your quotations for :-

1. 15 Doz. Tea Cups and Saucers
2. 12 Doz. Coffee Cups and Saucers
3. 20 Doz. Dinner Plates
4. 12 Doz. Small Glasses

30. Reply to Above

Dear Sirs,

We thank you for your letter No. -- dated the -[th] July. We submit below our quotations :-

1. 15 Doz. Tea Cups and Saucers at Rs. 40/- per Doz.
2. 12 Doz. Coffee Cups and Saucers at Rs. 60/- per Doz.
3. 20 Doz. Dinner Plates at Rs. 150/- Per Doz.
4. 12 Doz. Small Glasses at Rs. 60/- Per Doz.

Assuring you of our best services,

31. Reply to a Letter of Enquiry

Dear Sir,

We thank you for your enquiry of November, 20-- about our shoes. We are pleased to send you a copy of our illustrated catalogue and price-list. As you will find from these, we are manufacturers, exporters and wholesalers of all kinds of ladies, children, babies and gents shoes, sports shoes and sandals. Comfort and quality is the motto of our shoes.

We have sufficient supplies of our products in stock and can supply these within 8 days of receiving your order. We can also fill your order within 3 days on urgent basis. Our Mumbai representative would be pleased to call on you with some samples. We have instructed him to have an appointment with you on phone.

We look forward to the opportunity of having long-lasting and mutually beneficial business relations with you.

Thanks,

32. Enquiry about Ceramics

Dear Sir,

Ours is an Export House, and we export all types of crockery to South-East Asia.

We are interested in your tableware, particularly in bone hotel and zen china. We have a good export demand for tableware, hotelware, coffee mugs, and cups and saucers of good quality.

We want to give you a good trial order, and rely upon you to offer us good value in order to secure repeat future business. We may again remind you that these products are wanted exclusively for export. Therefore, send us immediately your quotations for your ceramics.

We hope you would put us on your very best terms as regards discount, incentive and payment.

33. Asking for a Price List

Dear Sirs,

We are interested in making purchases of various hosiery articles you deal in.

Since we are catering mainly to the middle class people, we are specially interested in medium priced goods of good quality.

We, therefore, request you kindly to send us a Price List, together with business terms.

34. Request for Price-List

Dear Sir,

We deal in various types of glasses and mirrors, like clear and tinted, float glass, sheet glass, figured glass, wired glass, and high quality mirrors, besides automobile safety glass. We represent a couple of well known glass companies like Asahi India, Atul Glass and Maharashtra Glass. Recently, we have received several enquiries about your products, specially about your figured glass in 12 designs.

Therefore, we want you to send us your latest catalogue and price-list along with samples, by your area representative. We can assure you of our repeat bulk orders if the prices and incentives are really competitive.

We hope to hear from you soon.

35. Reply to the Above

Dear Mr. Gurunath

We thank you for your letter of April, 20-- showing your keen interest in our glass products and requesting us for a price-list and catalogue. We are enclosing our latest catalogue and price-list; however, our Area Representative would call on you only after a week or so, as he has a very busy schedule for a couple of days. He will bring with him samples of our various products. He is authorised to discuss with you the discount, incentive etc. which are really very tempting.

We can assure you high quality of our products and prompt delivery of the same.

With thanks,

36. Enquiring about Goods Ordered from Abroad

Dear Sirs,

We wish to draw your attention to our order No. --, --/--/-- dated July -, 20-- (copy enclosed for ready reference).

The goods ordered for have not been supplied by you in five

months, though we understand that it should not take more than 2 months for goods to this kind to reach India.

Please look into the matter and inform us when we can expect these goods to be in our hands.

We need hardly emphasise the urgency, as we shall have to shore the goods for the next winter if they are received very late.

37. Sending Price List / Business Terms

Dear Sirs,

We have the pleasure to acknowledge your letter of December -- and to send you a Price List of the varieties we deal in.

We shall offer you trade discount of 10% on the articles worth Rs. 1000 and above. We can offer you 30 days credit facilities if you deposit a security of Rs. 20,000.

Assuring you of the best of our attention and co-operation.

38. Asking for an Estimate

Dear Sirs,

Could I have an estimate of redecoration and furnishing of my four room suite? The work will include oil painting of the walls and ceilings, and furnishing of one most modern drawing room and three bed-rooms with furniture, carpets and cushions.

Please send your representative to visit our house on prior appointment, and give us an idea of the time you will take to complete the work.

39. Sending an Estimate

Dear Sir,

We thank you for the kind courtesy shown to our representative who visited you in connection with redecoration and furnishing work.

Enclosed please find a detailed estimate of the entire work which we shall complete in three weeks.

Kindly instruct us, when you will like us to undertake the work.

Assuring you of the best of our attention.

40. Pre-Purchase Enquiries

Dear Sirs,

We have a stationery counter in our institution which supplies all items of stationery to our students at no profit basis, for which we propose to make bulk purchases of stationery for the years 199....

We shall be pleased to see your price list and know the special discount that you can offer.

41. Sending Price List

Dear Sir,

We thank you for your letter of December--.

Enclosed please find an exhaustive price list of various items of stationery.

Our prices are most competitive and we shall be pleased to offer you a special discount of 20% as a special case.

Assuring you of the best of our attention and cooperation.

42. Sending a Catalogue

Dear Sir,

Enclosed please find the latest catalogue of our publications which, we are sure, will greatly interest you.

We shall be able to offer you 25% trade discount with one month credit facility.

43. Enquiring about Cost of Trip

Dear Sirs,

We have read with interest your advertisement in the Times of India about the Vacation Trip to South-East Asia.

We shall appreciate, if you kindly send the detailed information about the cost of the trip, economy class and 1st class.

The above information is required for our Managing Director.

44. An Enquiry about Estimate on Renovation of a Showroom

Dear Sirs,

Subject : Estimate on Renovation of Showroom

We would be pleased if you could send us an estimate to renovate our showroom at the above address. The space to be renovated is shown in the plan enclosed. The details regarding specification of materials to be used are also attached.

We want that the renovation work is done at night and finished within 15 nights so that our showroom is closed to our clients and customers for minimum possible days.

We hope the time schedule would be strictly adhered to and the workmanship would be of acceptable standard and according to our specification.

You may send your civil engineer along with his assistant to inspect the place the next week for we want that the work is undertaken at the earliest.

Please let us know immediately whether you can undertake this job or not.

45. Asking for Samples and Price List

Dear Sir,

We deal in pesticides and chemicals related to agriculture and have a network of retail outlets throughout the country. We are interested in bulk purchase of your insecticide.

We have received several enquiries about this product of yours from many of our small and medium agricultural customers. We may place with you an immediate trial order if your prices are competitive. It may be mentioned that most of our clients are medium, small and marginal farmers, and their buying capacity is not high. Only moderately priced insecticide is required.

Therefore, we request you to send us the samples of the insecticide with your representative at the earliest. We hope you shall quote the lowest price you are prepared to accept.

We look forward to an early response and action.

46. After Sample Follow up Letter

Dear Mr. Prabhakar

We sent you a sample kit last week. Since we have not heard anything from you, we wonder if you have received the sample. We would like to know it, so as to send you another sample.

Perhaps you have been so occupied that you have not been able to open the packet. If this is so, please spare a few minutes of your valuable time and examine the contents of the interesting kit.

We shall greatly appreciate if you kindly drop us a line and let us know what you think about it.

47. Enquiring about Likely Increase in Advertising Rates

Dear Sirs,

We are anxious to know if you expect any further increase in the advertisement tariff next year.

The information sought will be of much use to us to plan our next year's publicity budget.

We shall greatly appreciate, if we are furnished with the necessary information at a very early date.

48. Reply to Above

Dear Sirs,

We thank you for your letter of January--

The advertising rates are likely to register a slight increase in view of the expected increase in the price of newsprint after the next budget. We anticipate about 12% increase in the rates of advertisement.

Nevertheless, the circulation of the leading newspapers has recently gone up and, thus, the higher rate of advertisement will be duly compensated.

49. Ordering Goods

Dear Sirs,

Please supply the following articles as early as possible by VVP :
1. 1 Pull Over - Full size.
2. 2 Cardigans (Ladies) - Medium Size

3. 6 Stockings - size 8

Since winter is running out an early dispatch of goods will be highly appreciated.

I am enclosing a cheque of Rs. 500 as an advance payment. The balance amount may be charged in the V.P.P.

50. Order for the Supply of Books

Dear Sir,

In response to your advertisement in the July issue of your catalogue for the sale of books, we would like to introduce ourselves as a leading supplier of books to the schools and colleges in Nagpur.

We want to purchase the following books :

1. Indian Politics - 100 copies.

2. Indian Economy - 150 copies.

3. Indian Geography - 125 copies.

4. Statistical Analysis - 75 copies.

We would like you to honour the following terms and conditions:

1. 10% special discount of bulk purchase.

2. Books must be delivered within a week.

3. If books are not in proper shape, we reserve the right to cancel the order.

4. Payment by cheque will follow the receipt of delivery.

Thanking you,

51. Order for Crockery

Dear Sirs,

We shall be glad if you will please send us the following goods by goods train, as per rate of your letter No. -- dated the --st July.

1. 15 Doz. Tea Cups and Saucers @ Rs. 40/- per doz.

2. 12 Doz. Coffee Cups and Saucers @ Rs. 160/- per doz.

3. 20 Doz. Dinner Plates @ Rs. 150/- per doz.

4. 12 Doz. Small Glasses @ Rs. 60/- per doz.

Please pack the goods as usual and collect the amount of invoice by negotiating the R/R through the state Bank of India.

52. Reply to Above

Dear Sirs,

We acknowledge with thanks your esteemed order No. -- dated the --st July.

The goods have been despatched to-day by goods train and R/R along with a copy a invoice has been sent to state Bank of India, Bandra branch, Mumbai.

Kindly arrange to collect R/R against payment.

Thanking you and assuring you of our best co-operation always.

53. Ordering Electrical Goods

Dear Sirs,

Please send us the following goods by passenger train, as early as possible :

1. Table Fans	 3
2. Ceiling Fans (48")	 2
3. Ceiling Fans (56")	 4
4. Electric Heaters - Model (A)	 6
5. Electric Heaters - Model (B)	 4

Kindly pack the goods as usual and draw hundi at 90 day's credit through the state Bank of India, camp, Pune.

54. Receipt of Order-Execution in Due Course

Dear Sirs,

We thank you for your Order No. – of – May, which we received this morning for fifteen cases of Indian Raw Silk. It is having our immediate attention and will be executed within the course of 15 days.

55. Placing Order after Making Enquiries on Telephone

Dear Sirs,

With reference to the conversations our Shri Mohan had with your Sales Organiser on the phone today, we confirm the order given to him and hope that you will execute the same as early as possible.

We enclose a written order for the goods required.

56. Acknowledging Receipt of an Order

Dear Sirs,

Please accept our thanks for your order No.-- of --th December for 14 (fourteen) cases of Copper Wire weighing 2019 kg. to be delivered to you by the first week of next month.

We have carefully noted your instructions.

We trust that our execution of this order will be to your complete satisfaction.

57. Regretting to Execute Order Immediately

Dear Sirs,

Thank you for your order dated – May 20--.

We regret to say that we are unable to execute the order within ten days, as desired. The demand for the goods has been so great for the last two months that the manufacturers who generally keep a big reserve stock have not a single piece left. They are working overtime at the mills to execute the orders, and the latest we can promise to deliver is beginning of July.

We are sorry to keep you waiting, as we know that you have reckoned upon these goods but the demand has exceeded all previous experience.

58. Acknowledgement of Orders - Wrong Price Stated Therein

Dear Sirs,

We acknowledge with thanks the receipt of your letter dated the -- October, placing an order for 20 Table fans.

We notice, however, that you order these at Rs. 750/- each. The correct price is Rs. 875/- and not Rs. 750/-. We feel this is just a typographical error. While we are getting your goods packed, we are writing this for your formal approval, on receipt of which we shall despatch the goods immediately.

Thanking you and assuring you of our best co-operation always.

59. Reply to Above

Dear Sirs,

We thank you for your letter dated October.

We confirm our order at Rs. 875/- each.

Please despatch the goods as early as possible and send your bill and R/R through the Bank of India.

60. Confirming a Part of the Order

Dear Sirs,

We thank you for your order dated – November 20--.

We shall be pleased to supply you items 1 to 32 at the prices mentioned by you. Regarding other 7 items we regret we are unable to supply the same at the prices quoted by you. We are, however, enclosing our latest catalogue showing lowest prices. Since you have desired the execution of your order in full, we are unable to send you the goods mentioned against S. Nos. 33 to 39. We shall, therefore, request you to please inform us telegraphically if we may despatch all the goods. On receipt of this information, we shall do the needful immediately.

Thanking you and assuring you of our best co-operation at all times.

61. Order for Books

Dear Sir,

Please send us the following books on our usual discount terms of 30% of published prices. These may be sent by Vishal Transport Company, and the documents may be forwarded through our bankers, State Bank of India branch.

Sr. No.	Number of Copies	Title	Author	Price Each Copy (Rs.)
1.	115	--	--	50.00
2.	125	--	--	75.00
3.	190	--	--	90.00
4.	201	--	---	40.00
5.	301	--	--	100.00
6.	101	--	--	60.00

We look forward to prompt delivery.
With thanks.

62. Order Based on Quotation

Dear Sir,

We thank you for your quotation of August, 20-- for your fire-protection products. We shall feel obliged if you supply us the following within 15 days of the receipt of this order :

10 Sprinkler Systems	Rs. 1,500.00 each
20 Extinguishers	Rs. 1,600.00 each
(Portable & Trolly Types)	
15 Fire Alarm Systems	Rs. 2,000.00 each

The above prices are inclusive of delivery expenses.

Please send these immediately, as they are urgently required by our customers. We hope you will respond immediately.

63. Refusing a Request for Additional Discount to a Buyer

Dear Sir,

Thank you for your letter of April, 20--, but we feel sorry that you find our quotation for our new wave AM/FM Pocket Radio on the higher side. We may reiterate that they are quite reasonable so as to allow you proper margins. Therefore, we are sorry not to allow any additional discount to our usual rate of 20%.

We may tell you frankly that soon there would be an upward revision in our prices, in view of the rising input costs. In fact, our prices are on the lower side and very competitive.

Our AM/FM Pocket Radio has never-before features like fully extended antenna. This telescopic antenna brings you crystal clear reception. The soft operating back-switch gives a wide range of adjustment. Besides, its plug-in 3.5 mm earphone gives you one-to-one intimate experience. Actually, there is much more than these.

You being our long customer, we would have not liked to refuse some additional discount, but in the prevailing circumstances, it is not practical at all. We hope you can appreciate our position. We think you will reconsider the matter and send us your order at the price we have quoted.

We look forward to your early order.

With thanks,

64. Refusing Execution of an Order

Dear Sir,

Thank you for your recent order No. -- of – December. 20 --, for 200 bags of cement. However, we are really sorry to say that we are not in a position to fill your order because of your strict condition of delivery of the consignment before 15ᵗʰ January.

Our inability to comply with your present order is because of your strict delivery schedule on urgent basis. Our products are in great demand and we already have large pending orders.

We can despatch you the above goods if you are willing to receive these by the end of January. We hope you will reconsider the matter, and give us sufficient time. In case you cannot do so, you may please try to meet your present urgent requirement from some other source.

65. Partial Execution of an Order

Dear Sirs,

Thank you for your Order No. -- of -- March 20.... In accordance with your present order, we have despatched all the items except that at Serial No. -- Code No. -- as it is at present out of stock.

We shall send the remaining items by the second week of next month as these would be readily available by then.

We have handed over the invoice, bill of lading and other relevant documents of Messrs.... and have instructed them to forward this consignment to you. This is insured against all risks and the forwarding agents, Messrs.... are authorised to recover all there dues from you.

With the consignment we have enclosed a number of our catalogues and price lists for distribution to your customers and patrons.

We hope you will receive all the articles in good condition as they have been very securely packed.

We look forward to another bulk order in near future.

66. A Follow up As The Orders Incomplete

Dear Sir,

Thank you for your order No. -- dated -- November, 20 --, Fridge, oven against our quotation No. -- of -- November, 20 --. We are ready to despatch these goods to your address as soon as possible but you have not mentioned the size of Venetian blinds, nor is there any mention as far as their colour/shade is concerned. I think it is because of a slip of mind. The specifications of all other items are there, and so, there is no problem.

For want of this specification, your order could not be processed. Therefore, please let us know by return of post, or on phone, the sizes and numbers of the Venetian Blinds you require now. You may indicate your requirement on the margin or bottom of this letter, and mail it back to me immediately, and I shall have your consignment ready in no time.

I look forward to your immediate response in this matter.

67. Cancelling an Order

Dear Sirs,

Kindly refer to our Order No. -- dated -- March for supply of electric heaters.

We have received a large consignment of electric heaters from one of our foreign suppliers and our shop is too full to accommodate more goods. We shall, therefore, feel obliged if you will please treat the order referred above as cancelled.

We realise that this will upset your arrangements for supplies but we are sure you will accommodate us in the circumstances in which we have been placed.

We shall be glad to reimburse you for any loss you might incur on account of our cancelling this order.

Assuring you of our best co-operation.

68. Cancelling an Order

Dear Sirs,

The above order was booked by your sales Representative, Shri Raman Kumar yesterday.

On re-checking our stock position we find that most of the good ordered by us are in our stock and we would not be needing the ordered goods in the near future. We, therefore, request you to please treat the order as cancelled.

We shall write you again when we need the goods.

Regretting very much for the inconvenience caused and assuring you of our best co-operation always.

69. Cancelling an Order-Delivery Time Expired

Gentlemen,

We beg to refer to our order dated – August, and request that the same may please be treated as cancelled as the date of delivery has expired since long.

70. Cancelling a Part of Order-Goods Received not Confirming to Sample

Dear Sirs,

While checking the goods received today we find that the same do not conform to the samples supplied by you. We, therefore, request you to please treat our order for the remaining 50 boxes as cancelled.

71. Request for Goods on Credit

Dear Sir,

Our almost 2 years old business dealings with you have been on cash basis, but now, with the expansion of our business and our repeat bulk orders to you, we find it very inconvenient, and so, would like to have goods from you on credit.

Therefore, we are enclosing our Order No. -- for worth Rs. 537,000 on charge account with bi-monthly settlement. This facility would save us a lot of inconvenience of making payments on each and every bill.

If you like, we may provide you a couple of excellent trade and bank references.

We look forward to your immediate and favourable response, as these goods are urgently needed.

With thanks,

72. Favourable Reply to Above

Dear Mr. Dalal,

Thanks for your order No. -- for LCD TV's and the letter requesting us for the transfer of your business from payment on bills to charge account.

Our business transactions with you have been quite satisfactory and they have now quite matured. Therefore, we are happy to grant you credit facilities, and from now, all your orders will be on charge account basis with 2 months' settlement period. Generally, we ask for references while granting these facilities, but in your case it is not required at all. We are fully satisfied as regards your creditworthiness and financial position.

Your present order is being processed and would be despatched soon.

We look forward to your bigger repeat orders.

73. Unfavourable Reply

Dear Sir,

Thank you for your letter of – February, 20-- accompanied by an order for LCD TV's. However, we are sorry to say that we cannot grant you charge account facilities, at least for the present, in spite of the fact that our business relations with you have been almost 2 years old.

To the best of our knowledge, your present financial obligations are already too heavy. It would be certainly not good for your financial health to transfer your business from cash basis to charge account terms at the juncture. In future, when you financial obligations are substantially reduced, you can again make a request for supply of goods on credit, and then, we would be glad to grant you this facility.

But you are most welcome to place your orders with us on cash basis, as you have been doing in the past. Therefore, we are not filling your present order and wait for your further instructions.

We hope you can appreciate our difficulty in not granting your request, although we would very much like to help you.

74. Supplier Asks for References

Dear Sir,

We are in receipt of your order No. -- Dt. -- March, 20-- for Filing Cabinets, Premium Executive Chairs and LapTop's on open account terms. But, we would like you to send us two sound trade references before we fill your order on credit. It is our old and well-established practice to ask for such references before granting these facilities.

We hope you would send us soon the names and addresses of two other reputed firms and suppliers with whom you have business on credit terms so as to enable us to execute your order at the earliest.

75. Reply to Above

Dear Sirs,

We thank you for your letter of – March, 20-- asking us to supply you trade references in order to grant us charge account business terms and facilities, with quarterly settlement.

We are pleased to give the following names and addresses for you to check our credit status :

1. --
2. --
3. --

We look forward to your early and fovourable response.

With thanks,

76. Supplier Takes Reference with a Trader

Dear Sirs,

M/s Ramchand & sons of Bandra (west) Mumbai have placed an order for good worth Rs. 35,000.00 for our products on credit, and have given your name as a reference.

We would feel obliged if you could advise us about this party's creditworthiness and financial status. Further, we would like to know how long these people have had an account with you.

We will treat any information received in this matter in strict confidence. A prepaid self-addressed envelope is enclosed for your convenience.

We look forward to your early reply so that me may take timely decision on extending credit facilities up to Rs. 35,000.00 to the party.

With thanks,

77. Trader's Favourable Reply

Dear Sir,

We are in receipt of your letter of – March, 20-- seeking status information about Ramchand & sons, Bandra (west) Mumbai.

We are glad to respond favourably, and wish to state that we don't hesitate to trust this party with goods worth any amount on credit. We have had business dealings with them for the last 5 years and there was not a single occasion when they gave us a cause to complain.

On the basis of our long experience with them we believe them to be highly creditworthy.

This information is given in strict confidence and without any responsibility on our part.

78. Trader's Unfavourable Reply

Dear Sir,

Reference your letter of -- March, 20--, seeking information about the financial soundness of the company in reference, we want to state that this party has not had much dealings with us.

Therefore, we are sorry to say that we are not in a position to give you the desired information regarding the party mentioned in your letter. Whatever limited business we had with them was on cash terms only.

In these circumstances, you will realise our inability to supply you required precise credit information.

79. Acknowledging Receipt of Goods

Dear Sirs,

We acknowledge with thank receipt of goods sent by you vide your consignment No.... dated....

We thank you for an early supply of the goods and express our satisfaction over the quality of the goods, with the hope that you will maintain it in your own business interest.

Enclosed please find a cheque of Rs. 50,000 in full settlement of the account.

Kindly acknowledge receipt.

80. Ordering Goods To be Supplied to a Third Party

Dear Sirs,

Please supply a Nokia E – 63, Mobile Phone in the name of Raj at the following address, on 2nd January 20-- :-

Shri Raj Patil

201 - A, Sarang Height, Nigdi, Pune - 411044

The Greeting Card, bearing my name, should accompany the phone to be delivered to the party some time in the morning.

Enclosed please find a cheque of Rs. 10,500/- towards the payment of the phone.

I shall appreciate, if you confirm the above instructions.

81. Asking for Goods on Approval

Dear Sirs,

We are interested in the sale of your goods on a agency basis. We shall, however, like to receive some samples of stocks on approval. This will enable us to display your goods and elicit popular response, before we finalise the terms of agency.

Assuring you of the best of our attention and cooperation.

82. Sending Goods on Approval

Dear Sirs,

We have the pleasure to receive your letter of – December 20--.

We shall be pleased to send you our goods on agency basis, subject to the terms enclosed.

In the meantime, we send you a package of some samples for your approval and display.

We trust, with your good salesmanship, you should be able to catch up a good business.

Assuring you of the best of our attention and cooperation.

83. Supplier Sends the Bill / Invoice

Dear Mr. Sumeet,

We are enclosing our Invoice No. -- for the redymade garments for men, women and children, supplied on -- June, 20-- against your above order.

New Age Fashion
30/2, Textile complex
SURAT, Gujrat

Phone : .....

INVOICE

Orient Dresses,
1009, sadashiv peth,
Tilak Road, Pune - 411030

Your Order No. --
Dated : -- June, 20 --

Invoice No. --

S. No.	Qty	Particulars	Unit Price Rs.	Total Rs.
1.	20	Ladies Suits (Silk)	700.00	14,000.00
2.	40	Gents Polyester Shirts (Classic)	300.00	12,000.00
3.	50	Neckties	60.00	3,000.00
4.	80	Cotton Frocks	40.00	3,200.00
5.	100	Woollen Socks (Pairs)	35.00	3,500.00
		Less 25% Total		35,700.00
				8,925.00
			Gross Total =	26,775.00

E & OE

84. Buyer Writes about Incorrect Trade Discount

Dear Mr. Rajesh shah

We are in receipt of your Invoice No. -- of -- June, 20-- but we have noted that it allows a trade discount of only 25% instead of 30% which you had agreed to on telephone on -- May, 20--, because it was a repeat, large order for garments.

Calculated on this Invoice gross total of Rs. 35,700.00 the difference is discount is precisely Rs. 178.50. Therefore, kindly adjust your bill accordingly and intimate us, and we shall pass the bill for immediate payment.

With thanks,

85. Supplier Sends Statement of Account

Dear Mr. Pandit,

Please find enclosed our statement of Account for the period January-February, 20--, amounting to Rs. ---- We have allowed you our usual trade discount of 30% on bi-monthly payment.

If you fail to pay the amount within a week of the receipt of this statement of Account, then reduce the rebate to 25% as has been agreed to in our trade terms.

We would feel obliged if the account is cleared and settled at the earliest.

With thanks,

Rainbow photo films
Veer Savarkar marg
Prabhadevi Mumbai - 400008

Phone : .....
-- March 20--

STATEMENT OF ACCOUNT
Panorama Studio,
Laxmi Road, Pune - 411030

Dates	Particulars	Debts Rs.	Credit Rs.	Balance Rs.
10.10...	Bill No. 765	1,550.00		1,550.00
15.10...	Bill No. 799	2,500.00		4,050.00
30.01...	Cheque received		3,000.00	1,050.00
02.02...	Debit Note JP - 110	1,50.00		1,200.00
10.02...	Bill No. 1507	2,000.00		3,200.00
25.02...	Bill No. 2000	4,000.00		7,200.00
27.02...	Credit Note JP - 25		200.00	7,000.00
	Less 30% (2 months)		2,100.00	4,900.00

86. Reminder to the Buyer for Payment

Dear Shri Raghavendra,

Our Account Section has reported that you have so far not cleared our Statement of Account No. -- of -- January, 20 --

You have always been prompt in clearing your accounts all these years, and so we wonder if it is because of oversight, or any other reason that your payment has become overdue. Anyhow, we request you to settle it soon.

In case you find the statement of Account in issue incorrect, or your have any objection to raise, please let us know by return post so that we may do our best to satisfy you.

We look forward to your immediate response and settlement of the account. We are again enclosing a copy of the Statement for your convenience.

With thanks,

87. Second Reminder for Payment

Dear Sir,

You must have received our earlier reminder of – April, 20--, on the subject noted above, but we regret your silence. We want to remind you again about our outstanding overdue for payment.

According to our trade terms, you have been allowed credit facility for 2 months only, but to our discomfort, we have found on many on occasion that payments have fallen overdue and our reminders have failed to have desired results. Although you have been our old customer, we wonder why, of late, you have failed to settle your account in stipulated time. This has resulted in lowering your credit rating and status.

In return of handsome discount and prompt execution of your orders we expect timely settlement of your account.

Please clear your account immediately.

With thanks,

88. Yet Another Reminder

Dear Sir,

Subject : Payment of Statement of

Account No. -- dated -- January for Rs. --

We wonder and regret very much that in spite of our three reminders on that above noted subject we have not received the payment. We are really at loss not to have any reply from you.

We cannot afford to wait any longer and therefore insist that your account should be immediately settled, or we shall be obliged to pass on the matter to our legal counsellor at your risk and cost.

However, we do hope you will help avoid taking legal steps, which neither of us would like, by sending your cheque per return.

89. Buyer Replies

Dear Mr. Merchant,

Thank you for your last Reminder of -- May, 20 -- sent under Registered Cover, regarding settlement of the Account No. -- dt. -- January, 20... I also acknowledge your earlier 2 Reminders, but am really sorry that I was not in a position either to send the payment or respond to your letters.

It so happened that I was involved in a serious car accident while returning home late in the evening of -- March, and was admitted to the hospital. However, I am now fit to walk and work, and have been discharged from the hospital only a week back. During these days, the shutters were down and there was no business, no correspondence at all.

I had to spend a stupendous amount of money on my treatment, operation and hospitalization. Moreover, there were no sales, no business. Consequently, I am in great financial strains these days. But, I want to assure you of my payment by the second week of July.

I hope you can appreciate my problems and bear with me till the middle of July. I am very much apologize for all this trouble and inconvenience.

90. Buyer Settles the Account

Dear Sir,

Further to your recent reminder asking us to settle our due account No. -- dt. -- September, 20--, I enclose a cheque for Rs. 35,200 towards full settlement of the above.

I am really sorry, and regret the delay in payment because I was out of the country, and had really forgotten to instruct for its payment in my absence. I returned the day before yesterday from a business trip abroad, and resumed the office work today only.

This delay in payment has been totally unintentional, and I sincerely apologize for it. I hope it has not caused you much inconvenience.

With thanks,

91. Supplier Suggests Payment in Installments

Dear Sir,

We thank you for your cheque for Rs. 15,000.00 only, in partial payment of the long overdue account No. -- The balance amount remaining due on your above account is now Rs. 35,000.00. We appreciate the problems being faced by you, and your desire to pay your debts at the earliest.

Since now you are in some financial straits, however temporary, and not in a position to pay the balance amount in immediate future, and have requested us for extension of time to pay, we suggest that you pay it in five equal installments of Rs. 7,000.00 each. You may send your cheques by the end of every month beginning from August, for 7 successive months.

We understand your present payment difficulties, and again appreciate your efforts to settle the account at the earliest. You have been our old and reliable customer, and so we suggest this scheme of payment of your debt in installments.

We hope it will help you a lot in overcoming your payment problems.

With best wishes and thanks once again.

92. Supplier Returns the Excess Amount

Dear Sir,

Thanks for your letter of -- April, 20--, accompanied by a cheque for Rs. 39,060.50 towards full settlement of your account No. --.

On checking the account, we found that there was an error in totalling in our Invoice No. -- of -- January, 20--, and that we had overcharged you by Rs. 199.50. Thus, we received Rs. 199.50 in excess from you. We thought it better to send a cheque for this amount instead of crediting it to your account to square it up.

We regret the error in calculation and the consequent inconvenience to you. Please accept our apologies.

With thanks, we look forward to your next order soon.

93. Collection Letter

Dear Sirs,

May we please call your attention to your account of Rs. -- which has evidently escaped your notice? We shall be glad if you will let us have be return of post your cheque to balance this.

94. Collection Letter

Dear Sirs,

We shall be glad to have your attention drawn to our account of Rs. -- which is now overdue, and for which a cheque by return of post will be esteemed.

95. Collection Letter

Dear Sirs,

While going through our accounts, our auditors have pointed our that a sum of Rs. -- for bill Nos. -- and -- is over due from you. As we have to close our accounts for the financial year ending 31st March, we shall feel much obliged if you will please let us have your cheque for Rs. -- by return of post.

We take this opportunity of thanking you once again for your patronage and assure you of our co-operation at all times.

96. Collection Letter

Dear Sirs,

May we please draw your attention to our letters dated -- August and -- September, regarding settlement of our account for Rs. -- which is now long overdue?

An early settlement will be very much appreciated.

Thanking you,

97. Collection Letter

Dear Sirs,

We are surprised to find that you have taken no notice of our letters dated -- August, -- September and -- September, requesting you for settlement of your accounts for Rs. --. As the amount is now very much overdue, we must insist the payment by -- October, at the latest.

98. Collection Letter

Dear Sirs,

We are sorry to find that you have not cared to settle you account for Rs. -- in spite of our writing you letters on -- August, -- September, - September and -- September. Under the circumstances, we are left with no other alternative except to demand an immediate payment of the amount due to us.

Should you fail to settle your account by -- October, we would be compelled to entrust the matter to our solicitors, with instruction to take the necessary steps for recovering the amount.

We trust you will not compel us to take this unpleasant step and spoil our business relations.

99. Collection Letter

Dear Sirs,

We are in receipt of your letter dated -- September, demanding an immediate payment.

We are sorry to inform you that the season has been too slack this time and we have hardly been able to dispose of 15% of the goods purchased by us. While we are trying our best to sell the goods at whatever little margin we can for settling your account, we request you to extend the time-limit up to -- December.

We are sure in view of our long relations and present temporary difficulties, your will comply with our request.

---

100. Collection Letter

Dear Sirs,

Referring to your letters of -- August, -- September and -- September, I am sorry to inform you that as I was indisposed for nearly two months, I was unable to sign any cheque and so payment could be made during this period. I am now enclosing a draft for Rs. -- in full and final settlement of your bill.

I regret very much this delay in settling your account and hope you will not mind it as it was beyond the circumstance of my control.

101. Collection Letter

Dear Sir,

Your credit standing is such a valuable asset that we should dislike to see it injured by your failure to pay your long past due balance of Rs. 3,500.00.

Not only your ability to secure more goods from us is at stake, but also your ability to secure credit from other sources which may come to us for a report about you.

We know you will understand the seriousness of this matter and will sent us your payments for full amount by return of post.

102. Collection Letter

Dear Sirs,

In view of the circumstances stated in your letter dated the -- July, we have pleasure in informing you that your proposal of remitting payment of Rs. 9,000 in 9 equal monthly installments has been accepted.

May we, therefore, request you to please send us a cheque for you first installment which falls due on -- July.

103. Collection Letter

Dear Sirs,

We regret, owing to a large number of outstanding, we have not been able to remit payment of your bill which fell due on -- March. We are expecting some major payments on -- March, and we hope, we shall be able to remit at least 75% of due payment by -- March. We hope you will find the same in order.

We thank you and assure you of our best co-operation always.

104. Application for Sole Agency

Dear Sirs,

With reference to your advertisement in today's 'The Tribune', for offering sole Agency for Mumbai, we have pleasure in informing you that we shall be willing to work as your sole agents for Gujarat and Maharashtra States, on the following terms and conditions :

1. Sole Agency - All Sales in the states of Gujarat and Maharashtra will be made through us only. Any order received by you will be passed on to us for execution.

2. Discount - You will offer us a minimum discount of 40% while we in turn will maintain 25% as fixed by you.

3. F.O.R. - All goods will be accepted F.O.R. Mumbai.

4. Unsold Goods - All unsold goods will be exchange able/returnable. The cost of freight for returning the goods will be paid by us.

5. Payment - All payments will be made by cheques drawn on a local bank of Bombay for which the bank charges will be payable by you only. Further the payments will be made within 60 days of the date of the bill.

6. Disputes - All disputes will be settled in Bombay Courts.

7. Termination of Agency - Either party has the right to terminate agency by giving three month's notice.

Incidentally we may add here that we are being offered the same terms and conditions by other suppliers also.

It hardly needs mention here that ours is one of the best organised business in Mumbai and we are giving very good sales to all other suppliers.

We hope you will find the above acceptable and shall offer us your Sole Agency for Gujarat and Maharashtra States.

Thanking you and assuring you of our best co-operation at all times,

105. Offering Sole Agency

Dear Sir,

    We thank you for your letter dated -- June, for the subject cited above.

    We shall be glad to offer you Sole Agency for Bombay on terms and conditions mentioned by you except with minor changes as below.

    Discount - We shall allow you a maximum discount of 35% and not 40% as desired by you.

    Minimum Order - We shall not execute any order for less than 150 copies.

    We hope you will find the above acceptable and shall send us your formal confirmation by return of post to enable us to get the agreement typed.

    Thanking you and assuring you of our best co-operation,

106. Reply to Above

Dear Sirs,

    We thank you for your letter dated the -- June, and have pleasure in confirming the modified terms and conditions for your Sole Agency in Mumbai. While you get the agreement typed, may we request you to please send us your catalogue and titles, meanwhile, to enable us to make out an order.

    Thanking You,

107. Encouraging a New Travelling Salesman

Dear Shri Pande,

    I am in receipt of your Weekly Report and I am sorry to find that you have not been able to do much at Nagpur especially after your getting a very good business at Pune. Please do not be discouraged and go ahead with the planned tour and work on the instructions I gave you before leaving this place. I am not at all unhappy with this report and I am sure a man with high calibre like that of yours must be successful in this line and it is with this confidence that I appointed you to this job knowing that you have no previous experience of this line.

    With best wishes and good luck at Mumbai and other places,

108. Applying for Agency

Dear Sir,

This has reference to your advertisement in the Lokmat of yesterday, in regard to appointment of stockists/distributors for your standard hardware items.

We are already sole distributors for many standard hardware items of some very reputed and established companies in the field. We have been in this business for the last 10 years, and so, possess long and excellent experience in distributing and marketing of these products. Recently, we have received some very good enquiries about your products.

We can develop a good market for your items, as well as we have very good business contacts in the line, in this area of the city. Moreover, we possess large storage capacity and showrooms here.

We can provide you a number of excellent trade and bank references. In the light of these facts, we hope you will be quite willing to appoint us as your sole distributors in this area of Maharashtra.

We look forward to your detailed terms and conditions in order to get the agency rights at the earliest.

Thanks,

109. To a Potential Agent / Distributor

Dear Sir,

We manufacture and export various types of rubber sports goods including sports balls, bladders, cricket-bat-rubber-grips, insertion sheets etc. of international quality and standard.

We want to appoint a stockist and distributor of these items in your part of Mumbai. We may appoint you our sole stockist and distributor in the area if you are really interested. We can assure you only the best from us.

Since you are dealing in similar sports items, you may send us your detailed proposals regarding the nature and extent of other agencies held, trade connections, three trade and bank references, and detailed terms of agreement.

We look forward to have your response soon so that we may proceed further in the matter.

Thanks

110. Reply to Above

Dear Sir,

Thank you for your letter of -- September, 20-- offering us sole agency and distributorship in the area of your sports goods. As you are aware, we are in this business for the last several years, and have large business contacts. As such, we are really interested in the offer, on the following terms and conditions :

1. That you will pay us 25% commission on annual sales amounting to Rs. 50,000 and 3% extra on sales exceeding this amount. The amount of commission will be settled annually on the occasion of Diwali.
2. That we shall deposit Rs. 40,000 with you or your bankers as security.
3. That we shall clear our account on quarterly basis, and credit facility would not go beyond Rs. 40,000. Therefore, in case where this limit of Rs. 40,000 is crossed, you would be entitled to send further documents through bank for immediate payment.
4. That all publicity and promotional material, including price-lists, brochures etc. will be supplied by you, at your expense. You would also publish information regarding our appointment as sole distributors and agents in this area.
5. That all orders sent to you will be executed promptly, of course, subject to the availability of stock.
6. That either party is at liberty to terminate the agency distributorship by giving 3 months notice in writing.
7. That disputes, if any, will be subject to Mumbai Courts only.

Meanwhile, you may take up references with the following firms and banks with whom we have had business transactions for the last many years :

(i) --
(ii) --
(iii) --

We hope the above terms and conditions, and references would be acceptable and satisfying.

We look forward to have mutually beneficial business relations with you in the near future.

111. Requesting for Increase in Commission

Dear Mr. Ajay Rampal,

We need not repeat that in spite of cut-throat competition, we have been quite successful in promoting phenomenal sales of your particularly time and date stamping machines and airline ticket validators among end-users. This has resulted in excellent growth of sales, and corresponding increase in profits. This has been possible only because of our untiring efforts and excellent business contacts. We had to exert our utmost to push through you products across the city and the neighbouring states. And still, we are not complacent at all.

But we are receiving the same old rates of commission which is quite inadequate in view of above factors, leading to much increase in our expenses. Therefore, we consider it quite reasonable to ask you for 3% increase in our commission with immediate effect.

We hope that you would appreciate our position, and willingly accede to our request of this modest rise in commission.

With thanks,

112. Reply to Above (Partly Favourable)

Dear Mr. Raghuvir

We are in receipt of your letter of -- March, -- and thank you for it. We again appreciate your vigorous efforts in popularising our time-recording equipment among the end-users. We also admit that there is much competition and it needs a lot of initiative, drive, efforts and determination to boost the sale of these products, but still we cannot grant your request in full. However, we increase your commission by 1% with immediate effect.

We would have been really pleased to grant you full increase of 3% in your commission as requested, but in spite of increase in sales, there has been pressure on the bottom line because of increased labour, input and power costs.

We hope this increase, though modest, would satisfy you. We want to assure you of our fullest co-operation and consideration in the matter, but are totally unable to grant you 3% increase in your commission. We

---

expect you to exert yourself still more to further increase the sale of our time-recording machines.

We may remind you that similar increase of 1% in commission would have to be given to our other distributors and sole agents. Denial of this to them would be totally unjust, for they are equally precious to us and their promotional efforts and exertions cannot be ignored.

113. Another Reply (Unfavourable)

Dear Mr. Raghuvir

Thank you for your letter of -- March, 20--. We once again appreciate your efforts in making our products popular in the face of tough competition from other manufacturers of time-recording machines and equipments. But we are still unable to grant you the requested increase of 3% in your commission. This is almost impossible, at least at present.

We have considered your request thoroughly, but we are sorry not to find it justified. It is against our well established policy to grant raise in commission so soon and to only one of our distributors. We don't want to set a bad precedent by agreeing to your request, as it would render our normal business with other agents and distributors difficult, if not impracticable. Moreover, there has been much pressure on our profit margins due to increase in cost of power, labour, raw material and devaluation of the Rupee. Thus, foreign currency and components have become very costly.

We want to assure you of our full co-operation and consideration in the matter, but we think, this is not the right opportunity to ask for an increase in commission.

114. Offering Services of a Forwarding Agent

Dear Sir,

As you might be aware, we are the leading clearing and forwarding agents in this part of the country, and serve more than 500 clients, of which 200 are from Pune alone. They include the names of big business houses and export firms of international standing.

We own a huge fleet of containers, trailers, trucks, lorries, tempos and three-wheelers, and employ more than 1000 people.

We collect the consignments from the very door-step, to be sent by rail, road, sea or air, and deliver the same at the consignee's door. Thus, our services are from door to door.

We can collect the parcels etc. within 3 hours from the time we receive your intimation. Our services are very quick, safe, easy and reliable. However, if by chance any goods are not booked or the booked goods are not delivered in time, for any reason whatsoever, they will be housed and stored in our godown at our own risk and cost, and the needful would be done the following day.

Our freight charges are really competitive and moderate, as you will see from the enclosed brochure. Therefore, we are confident that the same would be acceptable to you. Should you find our services interesting, please drop us a line, and our representative would soon call on you to discuss the matter in detail.

We look forward to your early response.

With thanks,

115. Enquiring about Freight-Rates

Dear Sir,

We are engaged in the manufacture and marketing of polyester blended suitings, shirtings and dress fabrics. We also manufacture partically oriented polyester filament yarn from PET chips. A large portion of our products is for export to the Middle East and Europe. For this purpose, we require the services of 3-4 containers to transport the above items from our mills in Surat to Mumbai Port.

The goods containing fabrics and yarn need to be packed and transported carefully, in well-secured containers. We need the transport almost every week. We will inform you 12 hours before the containers are required.

Therefore, we would like you to send your quotations for the above container service, initially for a period of 6 months commencing from -- November, 20--.

We look forward to hear from you soon.

116. Requesting for Redirection of Goods

Dear Sir,

We sent a parcel of medicines to Messrs Royal Pharma Chem Pvt. Ltd. Kolkata on -- March. -- against your Railway Receipt No. -- dt. -- March, 20--. The R/R and invoices in regard to this parcel were sent by us to the above company by V.P.P., as desired by the buyer, but surprisingly they have failed to honour the V.P.P.

Since they have failed to honour the above V.P.P., we request you to redirect the parcel to our address in Mumbai we are enclosing the R/R in original, and would pay all the charges on the delivery of the parcel.

With thanks,

117. Ordering Clearing Agents for Taking Goods

Dear Sirs,

Please arrange to collect five wooden boxes containing nails and screws for our sending the same to :

> Messrs. Ravikiran & Sons,
>
> P.M. Road,
>
> Belgum

through goods train.

Please deliver us the necessary R/R and your bill for payment immediately after you have despatched the goods.

118. To Railway Authorities Regarding Redirection of Goods

Dear Sir,

On -- January, 2010, we had sent a railway parcel addressed to SELF at Pune. The Railway receipt and invoices covering these goods were sent by us to Messrs. Ram Brothers in accordance with their instructions. As they have been unable to honour the R/R, please redirect the our above address in Nagpur. We shall pay the necessary charges on delivery.

Thanking you,

119. To Railway Authorities, Regarding Non-Receipt of Goods

Dear Sir,

A parcel containing books addressed in the name of Messrs. Royale Books, Solapur was handed over by us to you for sending the same to Solapur by passenger train vide your R/R No. AB. -- dated -- September.

The addressee informs us that the parcel has not been received at Solapur Station so far. As the parcel is urgently required by the party concerned, we request you to please immediately look into the matter and see that the same has not been miscarried to some other station.

120. Delivery Order to Clear Goods

Dear Sirs,

We are enclosing herewith R/R Nos. --, -- and -- duly endorsed in your favour and request you to please clear the goods from the Railway Authorities and arrange to deliver the same at your above address.

You may send us your bill as usual in duplicate and we shall arrange to send the cheque immediately on receipt of the same.

Thanking you,

121. Reply to Above

Dear Sirs,

We acknowledge the receipt of your letter dated the -- August along with three R/R's mentioned therein. The goods have been released and the same are being sent through our delivery man. Our Bill for Rs. 120/- is attached herewith in duplicate. Kindly arrange to hand over the cheque to the bearer.

Thanking you and assuring you of our best co-operation at all times.

122. Supplier Informs the Buyer about Despatch of Goods by Road

Dear Sir,

We are glad to inform you that today we have despatched your consignment by Jaipur Golden Transport Company, Mumbai. The consignment consists of 7 cases containing 3 xerox machines. 2 lamination machines and 3 sets of U.P.S.

The goods are well stacked, and insured against all risks. The transporter will recover all his dues from you. With the consignment, we have enclosed copies of invoice, other documents, and instructional and advertisement material. You are likely to receive these within a week. Please check all the items immediately on reaching, to ensure that there is no damage to the items. In case there is any damage inform us immediately and also the transporter.

We hope the consignment would reach you in perfect condition because the transporter is a reliable and trusted one.

We are also enclosing all relevant documents including our Bill No. -- dated -- November, 20-- for Rs. --

With thanks,

123. Requesting Railway Authorities to Cancel R/R

Dear Sir,

Last evening, we had booked a large parcel containing electronic components against the above R/R (PWB), for which a freight of Rs. 950.00 has been paid. The parcel is destined for Ahmedabad.

Late last night, we received a fax message from our clients M/S Abhishek Enterprises, Ahmedabad, informing us that their shop and showroom has been severely damaged in fire, and so, they would not need the electronic components booked against the above R/R(PWB).

Therefore, we have to request your to cancel the above noted PWB and to return the parcel to the bearer of this letter.

The R/R (PWB) is enclosed, in original. The freight money may also be returned to the bearer after deducting the due cancellation charges.

With thanks,

124. Enquiry about Position of Consignment

Dear Sir,

On -- November 20--, we sent you one R/R No. -- dated -- November, 20--, freight Rs. 3200 (paid) for 10 cases of leather garments, shoes and other items, for shipping to Delhi, Bhopal and Simla.

Our consignees from the above destinations have informed us that the goods have not reached them, nor have we heard any thing from you in spite of the lapse of over a month's time. It is a matter of concern for us, as our clients need the goods immediately.

We shall appreciate if you please let us know the exact position of these goods and when we may expect the documents.

We look forward to your immediate response and action in the matter.

With thanks,

125. Complaint about Defective Goods

Dear Sir,

Last month we received -- photographic films against our Order No. -- of -- March 20 --. We paid the bill vide our cheque No --, a photocopy of which is enclosed. But we regret to say that these films are defective and not giving satisfactory results at all.

There are many complaints from our customers, and I am enclosing one of these complaints. As the complaint mentions, the films are old, blurred and have hairy lines on them. Besides this written complaint, we are receiving a number of telephonic complaints. This is really unfortunate and regrettable.

We feel there is something wrong somewhere. We want that you immediately send us a replacement packet of films and take away the films still left with us out of this lot.

126. Reply to Above

Dear Sir,

We are really very sorry to learn from your complaint of -- April 20 -- about the problem you have been facing on account of defective photographic films supplied by us.

However, we are sending immediately a replacement packet containing -- rolls of these. We have ensured that these are free from any defect and completely satisfactory. Send us the remaining lot of defective films so that we may examine them in our laboratory to ascertain how these defects crept into our premium product.

To compensate you for the inconvenience we shall allow you --% special rebate on the purchase of these and adjust the same against your next order.

127. Refusing to Accept a Complaint

Dear Mr. Rajeev,

We have received your letter of -- March 20... complaining about inferior quality of goods. However, we have very well investigated the matter and found that your complaint is not justified. The slight difference in quality of these goods is really negligible and also unavoidable.

We have fully complied with your order both in letter and spirit; therefore, there is no question of any kind of compensation. From the same common lot, we have supplied these items to a number of our other customers and there is no complaint at all as regards their quality etc.

However, we do agree that there was some delay in the despatches of goods to you because of rush of orders on account of busy season. We regret this slight delay in delivery. But we cannot admit that this justifies your complaint and demand of compensation in the form of special discount over and above 30% we have already allowed you.

We hope for and insist upon settlement of your account in full in due course.

128. Complaining against Incorrect Accounts

Dear Sirs,

We are in receipt to of your statement of Accounts for December 20--. It shows the debit of Rs. 3,900 and it omits the conspicuous entry of credit of Rs. 5,000 paid by us on 21st September 20--.

The correct position of the account will show a credit of Rs. 1,100.

Please look into your records and rectify this mistake under intimation to us.

129. Acknowledging Mistake in Accounts

Dear Sirs,

We thank you for calling our attention to mistake in the accounts. The statement has been corrected. A revised statement is enclosed after making the necessary entries. The position given in your letter in correct.

Please accept our apology for the incovenience caused.

130. Complaint Regarding Wrong Statement

Dear Sir,

We have just received our statement for the period ending -- June, 20 -- on our charge Account No. --. The statement shows a purchase of 2 Eurotech human engineered office chairs for Rs. 12,500.00 each on -- May. 20-- but we are dead sure we didn't order any such chairs.

We have verified from our concerned officials and department that no such purchase was made. However, all the other items in the statement are correct.

Therefore, we are enclosing a cheque for Rs. 34775.00 I shall feel obliged if you immediately look into the matter, so that our account may be cleared and the mistake rectified.

131. Pointing out Error in Despatch of Goods

Dear Sirs,

Please refer to your R. R. No... dated.... sending a consignment of silk sarees.

It appears, you have only partly met our requirements, and you have completed the rest of the order by sending us Sarees at random.

We regret to say, these Sarees, which were not ordered for by us, are, of no use to us.

We are, therefore, reluctantly sending them back at your cost, and request you kindly to complete our order at an early date.

132. Supplier's Complaint about Long Credit

Dear Mr. Singhania,

Our accounts department has reported that you have been clearing your debts after 3 or 4 months, instead of the stipulated on month. We had agreed to supply you our products on the clear understanding of 30 days credit, but you have been violating it. It is against our well-established policy and business conduct, and we hope that you would strictly adhere to it.

However, we do not mind such late payments, but then we cannot allow you the special discount of 3% over and above the usual trade discount of 25%. This special rebate is given only for monthly clearance of the bills. If you want to continue to avail of this special rebate, please see that your debts are cleared within the agreed period. In any case, the choice is yours.

We look forward to hear soon from you.

133. Complaint to the Post Office for the Goods Damaged

Dear Sir,

We seek to lodge a complaint that the package received by us, on December -- from Mumbai is badly damaged.

The package contained packing slips which have been received in a shocking condition. The outer wrappings were torn and mutilated and the inner contents were soiled.

It seems the package was tampered with by some one who ripped it open and dragged it through the mud.

Since the items in the package are for sale and these have been rendered so soiled that it is absolutely out of question to sell them, we are constrained to claim the damages which amount to Rs. 2500 as per the bill (copy enclosed).

It is requested that our claim for the damages caused by the negligence of the postal staff may please be passed and sent to us at an early date.

134. Acknowledging Complaint of Damages

Dear Sir,

I acknowledge receipt of your letter of December -- 20.... pointing out delivery of a damaged package.

We are sorry to learn it. But the Post Office cannot accept the liability for damages of any package unless it is insured.

However, we shall try to do our best to look into the matter, and we shall consider your request for payment of damages, if it is established that the damage was caused due to the negligence of the postal staff in handling it.

In the meantime, the enclosed form may please be sent to us duly filled in.

135. Complaint about Defective Umbrellas

Dear Sir,

I am aware of your good reputation for quality goods and reliability, and that is why I sent you and order for 500 quality, folding fashion umbrellas. I received the consignment last week and have sold a number of them of date. But I am sorry to say that there have been many complaints during these two-three days about these umbrellas from our customers.

The umbrellas supplied do not open smoothly, and there is also trouble when they are being folded. A number of umbrellas have broken ribs. It seems there is some manufacturing defect which has escaped scrutiny and inspection.

Certainly, there is something wrong with these umbrellas. Therefore, I request you to send us immediately a replacement consignment and take away the umbrellas still left with me out of this lot.

I hope you would take immediate suitable steps, seeing the urgency of the matter as it is rainy season and I need the replacements at the earliest.

136. Reply to Above

Dear Sir,

We are in receipt of your complaint of -- July, 20-- regarding defects in our umbrellas supplied to you against your Order No. -- of -- June, 20- -. We are really sorry to learn about the problem you have been facing on account of defective umbrellas received by you. But, at the same time, we are surprised to know about these defects, as these are our premium products and undergo strict quality control and check before supply.

However, we have ordered an enquiry to ascertain how it happened and who is responsible. Meanwhile, we are sending immediately a replacement consignment containing 500 fashion umbrellas. We have ensured that these are free from any defect, and completely satisfactory. Our representative would call on you sometime next month to collect the remaining lot of the defective umbrellas.

We propose to compensate you for this inconvenience by allowing you an additional discount of 2% on purchases made in your next order.

137. Complaint about Non-Delivery of Goods

Dear Sir,

I am sorry to state that you have so far not delivered the electrical appliances ordered by us vide our order No. -- on -- December, 20--, which was duly acknowledged by you on December, 20-- In this letter, you had promised immediate delivery of goods, but now almost 23 days have elapsed since then, and yet we have not received the advice of delivery.

Please arrange to send the consignment latest by -- January, 20--, or we shall be obliged to cancel our order and obtain these items from some other source.

We sent you this trial order only on the understanding that you would send the goods immediately. This delay in despatch of goods has caused us a lot of inconvenience and embarrassment.

We look forward to your quick response and action in the matter.

138. Complaint about Receipt of Different Goods

Dear Sir,

Having got released the documents from our bankers, we took delivery of the consignment, but to our great surprise, on opening the boxes we found different items. They do not tally with our order at all.

We had ordered 12 pieces each of wet and dry vacuum cleaners, but the consignment contained food-processors and grinder-mixer-cum-juicers. The value of these items is much more than the amount paid by us against our order. However, we would like to have these exchanged immediately with our ordered items.

Please arrange immediately for the supply of items ordered by us as they are urgently needed. Also inform us what you would like us to do with the present consignment, as we cannot hold these goods for a long time in our godown owing to limited space there.

We have spent Rs. 500.00 for carting this consignment to our godown. This amount may please be credited to our account.

We look forward to your immediate response and action in the matter.

Thanks,

139. Reply to Above Complaint

Dear Mr. Pathak,

We are in receipt of your letter dated -- April, 20-- complaining about receipt of wrong items and consignment. We are really sorry for this mistake and mix-up, and sincerely apologize. We hope this has not caused you much inconvenience.

Actually, this consignment was meant for another party in Delhi itself, but because of wrong marking of R/R Nos. by the Railway staff, the two consignments got exchanged with each other. We have received a similar complaint from the other party in Nagpur as well.

However, our sales representative in Nagpur has been instructed on phone to do the needful immediately. He will see to it that your consignment is delivered to your within a day or two. Please bear with us till then.

The amount of Rs. 500.00 has been credited to your account, and will be adjusted in the next bill. We again express our sincere apologies for the trouble caused to you.

140. Complaint about Goods Received in Excess

Dear Sir,

We thank you for prompt execution of our order No. -- dated -- February, 20--. We received the consignment containing 750 classic Melamine full plates, 400 Meridian cup-saucers and 400 coffee mugs far in excess of our order. We had ordered 300 full plates, 250 cup-saucers and 150 coffee mugs only, along with other tableware which have been found as per our order and specification.

We have been in business with you almost for a decade, and it is for the first time that such a mistake has occurred. It seems it must have taken place while collecting the items for our consignment. In a normal course, we could have asked you to send us a new bill for these items in excess, but our present requirement of these items is so fully met with that we are sorry not to ask for a new bill. Moreover, it is not prudent to block money and space for this surplus stock.

Pending your instructions as to how these items should be returned to you, we are holding these with us.

141. Complaint for Non-execution of Order

Dear Sirs,

We had placed with you an order for ten dozen special mixed toys which was confirmed by you about a month back promising the delivery within a week's time. So far the goods have not reached us and this has resulted in a considerable loss of business to us. If the goods have not already been despatched, please despatch the same within 4 days and wire us accordingly. If we do not hear from you within a week, we shall be obliged to cancel the order.

142. Reply to Above

Dear Sirs,

We thank you for your letter dated ___ and confirm our Telegram today which reads as below :

"Goods Despatched Today (.) Letter Follows"

We regret very much for the delay in executing your order but we may assure you that this was unavoidable as we had quite a large number of orders pending for execution. Inspite of our best efforts we could not despatch your goods earlier than today. We hope you will excuse us for the inconvenience caused and shall given us all support as in the past. We may add here that only yesterday we have appointed two more packers are chances for delayed execution, in future, will be the minimum.

We thank you and assure you of our best co-operation always.

143. Complaint Regarding Damaged Goods - Asking for Necessary Credit

Dear Sirs,

We thank you for the consignment of cabinets received against our Order No. -- dated -- Oct. We are much obliged for the prompt supply of goods.

However, on opening the parcels, we find that as many as 13 are in damaged condition and hence they are not saleable here. While we shall be returning these glasses in due course, we request you to please credit the amount of 13 cabinets to our account.

144. Reply to Above

We thank you for your letter dated -- October.

The consignment of cabinets was sent as per instructions contained in your order No. -- 'Ordinary Packing'. As intimated earlier, goods under ordinary packing are sometimes liable to be damaged owing to mishandling by Railway people and as such we have always suggested our customers to have goods in special packing of wooden cases. It costs a little more than ordinary packing but the chances of damaging the goods are minimised.

Although we are not liable to pay any such damages to you, we would, however, suggest you that you may please send us those thirteen cabinets and we shall get the same repaired at our cost this time. We may add here that we shall not entertain any such claim in future unless the goods are procured under special packing of wooden cases.

Thanking you and assuring you of our best co-operation always.

145. Reply to Above - Another Form of Letter

Dear Sirs,

We thank you for your letter dated -- October. The consignment of cabinets was sent as per instructions contained in your order No. -- 'Ordinary Packing.' As intimated earlier, goods under ordinary packing are sometimes liable to be damaged owing to mishandling by Railway people and for this purpose we always suggest our customers to procure goods under packing of wooden cases. No doubt, the wooden packing is slightly costlier but then it saves many complications.

As a special case we are issuing you a credit note for the damaged goods, but regret our inability to entertain any such claim in future.

We hope you will appreciate our point of view and shall advise us to send the goods under wooden packing as and when you order them again.

Thanking you,

146. Complaint to Railway Authorities for Non-receipt of Goods

Dear Sir,

Two parcels containing printed books were handed over by M/s. India Book House, to Railway authorities, for despatching the same by train to Mumbai-CST -- June.

The parcels have not reached till today and our business has been very much affected as the parcel contained books wroth Rs. 13000/- which were urgently needed for supply to our retail dealers. We, therefore, request you to please check up the availability of goods and let us know within a week's time so that we may submit necessary claim in case the goods are not traceable with you.

R/R against which the goods were booked bears No. -- dated -- June

Thanking you,

147. Reply to Above

Dear Sirs,

With reference to your letter dated the -- August, please send us R/R and invoice in original from the party in support of your claim.

148. Submitting R/R and Bill

Dear Sir,

We thank you for your letter dated -- August.

R/R No. -- and Bill No. -- for Rs. 13000/- from Messrs. India Book House, Kolkata are attached in original.

Please arrange to remit us the amount at your earliest.

Thanking you,

149. Remittance of Payment by Railway Authorities

Dear Sirs,

Enclosed please find Cheque No. -- dated -- September, for Rs. 13000/- (Rupees Thirteen thousand) in full and final settlement of your claim dated the -- August.

Kindly send us your office stamp receipt for the amount.

150. Sending Necessary Receipts for the Cheque

Dear Sir,

We acknowledge with thanks the receipt of your letter dated - September, along with a cheque for Rs. 13000/-.

Our official stamped receipt for the amount is attached.

Thanking you,

151. Complaint against Excess Bill

Dear Sir,

I have received my Electricity Bill for Rs. 1800 for a period of 2 months.

The bill appears to be inflated, as I know for certain that our consumption of electricity is not so high as to warrant such a high bill.

I, therefore, wish to get the meter checked at my cost, as early as possible.

152. Complaint to the Railways against Non-Receipt of Goods by the Buyer

Dear Sir,

We despatched a railway parcel by passenger train on -- June. 20- - against your Railway Receipt No. -- of the same date.

The parcel contained leather goods and was addressed to M/s O.B. Marketing Pvt. Ltd., M.G. Road. Pune It is more than 16 days back that we despatched this parcel. The consignees have informed us today on phone that the goods, which are urgently required for display in an exhibition have not reached them so far. We wonder whether the parcel has been miscarried.

We would, therefore, request you to make immediate enquiries into the matter and let us have prompt response. We are really anxious about the parcel because its contents are our new and premium products, meant for display in an exhibition by our consignees.

We look forward to your prompt action and reply in the matter. We are enclosing a photocopy of the above Railway Receipt.

153. Complaint against Frequent Breakdowns of Electricity

Dear Sir,

We, the residents of Maliwada, Ahmed Nagar want to bring it to your kind notice that during the last three months the supply of electricity in our locality is very irregular. The frequent breakdowns of the electric supply are causing a lot of inconvenience and trouble to the residents. The studies of the children are suffering as they are unable to read in the night time especially during their examination days.

We request you to kindly look into the matter immediately and ensure that there are no more breakdowns in future.

Thanking you,

154. To the Post Master Regarding Non-Delivery of a Money Order

Sir,

I sent a money order for Rs. 1500 vide Receipt No. -- dated -- February 20... From your Post Office. The money order was to be delivered to Mr. Vijay Kumar, 25, Senapati Bapat Marg, Pune. But I am sorry to inform you that the money order has not reached the addressee so far. I, therefore request you to kindly look into the matter and arrange for the prompt delivery of the money order.

Hoping to get an early reply in the matter.

Thanking you,

155. To the Inspector of Police Complaining Against the Loudspeaker Nuisance

Dear Sir,

I would like to draw your attention to the growing abuse of

loudspeakers in our area.

Loudspeakers are used without the least thought being given to the hardships caused to the people in general and students in particular. The constant blare of the loudspeakers drives students like me crazy and does not allow us to study peacefully. Our examinations are fast approaching and, hence, we need to study hard for them.

I, therefore, earnestly appeal to you to take prompt measures to put an end to this nuisance.

156. To the Corporator Complaining about the Nuisance Caused by Stray Dogs

Dear Sir,

On behalf of the residents of Dwarka, sect. I. I wish to draw your attention to the nuisance caused by stray dogs in our locality. We have written several letters of complaint to the various authorities in the Corporation and even to the Police Commissioner, but no action has been taken so far.

As we are all aware, the animal lovers' protest resulted in the disappearance of 'dog-catcher' vans earlier run by the municipality. At the same time, the sterilization programme introduced in lieu of that did not achieve any tangible result. Now the even increasing number of the stray dogs has really become a threat to the peaceful life of the people in the locality. There have been two incidents where dogs have bitten people and they have had to visit doctors for inoculations against hydrophobia.

The worst is at nights, when a pack of dogs sets up a continuous barking for no rhyme or reason. The situation is quite out of control and only action from the local authorities can ease our difficulty.

Kindly arrange for something to be done at the earliest, because this is a very serious problem that we have to face day and night.

157. Thanks for Service

Dear Mr. Shekhawat

Back home I am in my office once again. It was very kind of you to treat me so royally while I stayed with you for a week. The pleasant memories of the happy hours I spent in your company will ever haunt me.

I wish I could repay at least some of this generous hospitality of yours. My sense of gratitude for you increases all the more when I realize how busy you were and still how generously you spent time for me.

I am highly thankful for all that you did to make my business trip and stay there in simla so successful, comfortable and joyous.

158. Thanks for Prompt Execution of an Order

Dear Sirs,

Thank you very much for so prompt an execution of our Order No. -- of -- March. I am writing this letter to express my happiness and thanks. This promptness in despatch and delivery has helped us a lot in keeping our customers well satisfied. It has also helped us to make these items more popular.

I hope orders in future will also receive the same prompt and careful attention.

Thank you once again,

159. Regretting an Oversight

Dear Sir,

I received your letter of -- May yesterday complaining the non-receipt of goods against your Order No. -- of -- April. On checking our correspondence, I observed that I had mistaken the date of despatch. I regret the oversight. The fault is entirely mine and I sincerely apologise for the inconvenience caused to you.

By the time you receive this letter the consignment should have reached you. Moreover, to compensate you I have sent the goods on my expense. I hope this should satisfy you.

I once again apologise for the oversight resulting in inconvenience to you.

160. Thanks for Giving a Reference

Dear Sir,

I am writing this letter to tell you how pleased and thankful I am for taking up my trade reference and sending a favourable response to my supplier. Consequently, now I have credit facilities for any amount of order on my open account.

I am really most obliged for this favour and look forward to an opportunity to reciprocate it.

I thank you once again.

161. Acknowledging Note of Sympathy from a Business Party

Dear Mr. Sharma,

We appreciate your very kind message of sympathy expressed on the sad demise of Mr. Patil, our Sales Manager.

His death was a bolt from the blue, from which it will take us some time to recover. He was really a great asset to us, and we know the loss we have to suffer on his sudden parting.

We thank you very much for letting us know how you felt about him.

162. Congratulations on Marriage of Son

Dear Ravindra,

I am really very happy, and so are my associates here at silver Motors, to know about your eldest son's marriage. Our heartiest congratulations on the occasion. Convey my blessings to the newly-wedded couple.

I had received the marriage and reception invitation, but on the days of the marriage and reception, I was out of station, and so feel sorry to have missed the happy occasion.

Once again my warm congratulations.

163. Congratulations on Promotion

Dear Mr. Shukla,

Let me add my heartiest congratulations to the several others you might be receiving, on being promoted to the post of Executive Senior President in the company. Now you will be incharge of total operations of the complex. This has also increased your responsibilities further. But, for a man like you with so much experience, qualification and expertise, it is no burden at all. Moreover, you have an aptitude for challenging jobs which involve team management, leadership, efficient co-ordination and administration in a large organisation.

I came to know of this happy news while looking through a corporate magazine yesterday. You long deserved it, and so it gratifies me very much that now you have been suitably rewarded, though somewhat belatedly.

With best wishes for further promotion in near future.

164. Congratulations on Moving to a Better Office Premises

Dear Mr. Salve,

Heartiest congratulations on your moving to this new and so prestigious address. I came to know of it only today, when my eyes caught sight of your notice about the change of address in the Lokmat.

This new office premises has great locational advantages from many angles. This prime and prestigious location will go a long way in increasing your business activities manyfold. You very well deserved this premises. Your watch spectrum is already a leading product, in fact, a Numero Uno brand item.

Therefore, it is natural and desirable that you should have moved to such a splendid premises. Your technical collaboration with one of the first Fortune 500 multinationals has helped you a lot in achieving phenomenal and envious growth in business.

I wish you still better results and higher turnover in your business.

165. Acknowledging Congratulations

Dear Mr. Nagendra,

Thank you so much for your letter of congratulations and good wishes to me for receiving this year's Magna Excellence Award for Management Consultancy. It is really very nice of you to felicitate me on this happy occasion.

It is because of good wishes and blessings of friends, relations and well wishers like you that I have now got applause and acclaim, both from business barons and the powers that be. It is the congratulations and good wishes of the people like you, who really inspire me to fare forward more vigorously in the field of management consultancy.

Thank you once again,

166. Thanks for Giving Favourable Reference

Dear Sir,

Thank for your favourable reference to M/s Logitech services D-1, Gultekdi Ind. Area Pune. It is very kind of your to say that in your opinion we are highly reputable, financially sound and well-established people. Your favourable and so appreciable reference, in response to the status enquiry about us from the above firm, has been much helpful in seeking supply of goods on long-term credit.

We shall always remain obliged for this favour, and would like to reciprocate whenever there is such an opportunity.

With thanks and good wishes,

167. Thanks for Prompt Settlement of Accounts

Dear Sir,

It is to thank you for your prompt and timely settlement of our accounts during the last over two years. we very much appreciate your sincerity to your commitments, especially because a couple of these orders have been for huge amounts.

Time has helped us a lot to adhere to our own commitments of payments, and implementation of our projects an planned. It is buyers like you on whom we can bank upon for smooth functioning of our business.

We thank you once again, and look forward to the same co-operation and confidence in us as regards our future business relations.

168. Regretting Price-Increase

Dear Sir,

We wish to inform you that we have increased the prices of our Bopp Tapes, both plain and printed, by 15% with effect from --- January, 20--. We are enclosing our new price-list. We regret this increase, which has been rather overdue, in view of the higher costs of input, labour, power, overhead charges and sharp devaluation of Rupee in relation to Japanese Yen.

However, we have limited this rise in our prices to the minimum possible by absorbing much of the costs, by economising in other sections like conservation of energy, recycling of waste material to produce energy, and indigenising of the production to a great extent.

We hope you appreciate our position, and excuse this modest rise in the price of our products.

169. Sympathy to a Business-Associate

Dear Mr. Rajesh

I was very much distressed and grieved to know that one of your godowns got completely destroyed in the recent devastating fire. Thank God, it was adequately insured and there was no loss of life. But it is certainly a setback to your business, however temporary.

I wonder if I can be of any help at this juncture. You are welcome to inform me if I can do something for you. I hope the loss is less than has been reported in the newspapers.

I am with you in this hour of your loss and grief, and send my heartfelt sympathy.

170. Condolence to an Employee

My dear Ramesh,

I was shocked and stunned to learn about your beloved wife's sudden death, from our foreman today. The tragic news is so sudden and shocking that none of us here is ready to believe it.

She was so young and popular among the wives of our workforce, being a great social worker. I know you will miss her much, but I hope that the love you shared with her will help comfort you in the days to come. We all are with you in this hour of gloom and despair, and our deepest sympathy goes out to you. You must take heart, and bear it mainly for the sake of your only son Nitin. And he is still quite young. How would he, a little pretty soul, face it?

May God rest her soul in perfect peace and beatitude. Please do not worry about your absence, or work here. I shall get it managed. Please do inform me if there is anything I can do in this hour of crisis.

With my sincere condolences,

171. Thanks for Hospitality and Favour

Dear Ranjeet,

Back home, and I am once again in my office directing all the activities of the company. But I don't know how to thank you for making my business trip to Delhi so successful and happy. In spite of your awfully busy schedule as the Chief Managing Director of such a big organisation, you accompanied me to many offices and introduced me to so many captains of the business there, particularly in the line of cables.

It is only because of you that I could manage to secure such a large order for our products, and on so favourable terms. I wish I could repay at least a fraction of this hospitality and favour shown to me. My sense of gratitude increases all the more when I realize how your wife did all her best to make my stay at your residence so memorable and comfortable.

I am highly thankful to both of you.

172. An Apologetical Letter to a Customer

Dear Mr. Sane,

We are sorry to learn that the other day you returned from our Show-Room quite annoyed at the behaviour of the sales assistant.

We wish you had brought this to our notice immediately. That could have made things easier for us to put amends to the wrong done without any loss of time.

While we regret the inconvenience caused to you, we shall request you quite earnestly to give us another chance to serve you. We assure you of the best of our courtesy, and we are sure you will change your impression about us very soon.

Assuring you of the best of our attention.

173. Thanking a Paper for a Book-Review

Dear Sir,

I thank you very much for your most complimentary mention of my book Indian Economy in your esteemed columns last Sunday.

I am sure, the fact that the book has won your attention and commendation will enhance its demand.

My publishers also join me in thanking you for your kind consideration.

174. After a Foreign Business Visit

Dear Sir,

Reaching India, on my first day in my Office, the first thing that I wish to do is to express my deep sense of gratitude to you for your courteous behaviour and inspiring company, the sweet memories of which I still cherish in my mind.

I greatly appreciate your thoughtfulness in arranging my visit to your plant and offices and making business talks meaningful and mutually useful.

I hope, before long, you will visit India on a business tour and give me an opportunity to reciprocate your friendliness.

175. Soliciting Order from Old Customers

Dear Sir,

We have recently been through our records, and we are very sorry to find that for a considerable long time we have not received any order from you.

Since we have had no complaint from you, we assume you must have been fully satisfied with them. However, it is quite possible you might have felt some dissatisfaction somewhere of which you have not deemed fit to apprise us of. If this is so, we shall be very glad to have an opportunity of looking into the matter in our keen desire to serve our customers wholeheartedly.

We have recently extended our business and taken several new lines. Thus, we feel prompted to send you our list of articles which we offer to sell to you at 10% discount.

We sincerely hope, we shall have the pleasure of executing your renewed orders which, we assure you, will receive our fullest attention.

176. Credit Enquiry to a Bank

Dear Sir,

M/s Ramlal & Sons, Dadar circle, Mumbai have placed an order with us for our products worth Rs. 35,000/- on charge account business terms with quarterly settlement and have given your name as a reference.

We would feel obliged if you can give us information in regard to this party's status, financial soundness and creditworthiness. We would specially like to know how long this party has had accounts with you and whether any debts have been overdue. Please oblige us with any further information you have in this matter.

We may assure you that all this information given to us will be treated as strictly secret and confidential. A prepaid, self-addressed envelope is enclosed for your convenience.

We look forward to your early reply.

With thanks,

177. Bank's Favourable Reply

Dear Sir,

Thank you for your letter of -- March, seeking status enquiry about the company referred to in your above letter.

We are pleased to inform you that Ramlal & Sons, Dadar Circle, Mumbai have had current and deposit accounts with us for the last 6 years. Their accounts have always been in order, with sufficient balance to cover all their withdrawals.

They have borrowed money from us many times for short and long durations, ranging from Rs. 24,000.00 to Rs. 60,000.00, and have never been defaulters, in repaying their debts and interests well in time. To the best of our knowledge and information, there is no outstanding debt against them.

This party is good and reputable and their creditworthiness is beyond reproach.

In our opinion, there should be no hitch in extending credit facilities for any amount to this firm.

This information is given in strict confidence and without any responsibility on our part.

178. Introducing a Customer to an Agent Abroad

Dear Sirs,

I have the pleasure to introduce our esteemed customer Mr. H. Prabhakar who intends staying at London for sometime.

Since he has no acquaintance at London, we shall appreciate if you kindly provide him with necessary introductions and render him all possible assistance.

179. To a Customer Protesting against the Charges

Dear Sirs,

We have received your letter of – December 20, and regret that you consider a small charge made by the Bank to your accounts as unjustified.

You will please appreciate that during the last six months you have maintained a very small balance but still we have always valued your account. We shall therefore advise you to maintain a large balance which will save you of much inconvenience.

Assuring you of the best of our attention.

180. Asking Secretary of a Company to Supply Particulars for Opening an Account

Dear Sir,

I thank you for your letter of January -- 20--. Before opening an account in the name of your company, you are required to furnish the bank with a copy of the Constitution of the Company, together with a copy of the resolution and instructions for the mode of operation of the account.

181. To a Customer Who Endorses His Company's Cheques to His Personal Account

Dear Sir,

It has been noticed that you have often endorsed the cheques drawn to the order of your Company and paid them in for the credit of your private account, although you have not been authorised to do so.

This is a wrong practice though some of your personal cheques are made payable to the company.

Since this exposes the Bank to a great risk, I shall request you to operate the accounts in accordance with the rules of the Bank.

182. Asking the Bank for Statement of Accounts

Dear Sirs,

Reference your letter dated – Jan. -- 20... regarding over draft.

We would request you to furnish us with a statement of accounts to enable us to check up the accounts.

183. Pointing Out a Wrong Bank Statement

Dear Sir,

We are in receipt of Statement of Accounts covering deposit and withdrawals for the quarter ending – December 20...

The Statement contains a number of errors as outlined below :-
1. Deposit on Sept. - of Rs. -- is not shown.
2. A cancelled cheque of Rs. -- has been shown in the debit.
3. A withdrawal of Rs. -- has been shown on Dec. -- while the actual withdrawal is only Rs. --

Please rectify the entries and send us a revised statement of accounts.

184. Regretting the Erroneous Statement of Accounts

Dear Sirs,

We thank you for your letter of – Jan.-- 20--.

Your account has been reverified, and a revised Statement of Accounts in enclosed.

We are sorry for a wrong statement of accounts which has slipped from our hands.

185. Information to Bank about Inclusion of Another Partner in the Company

Dear Sir,

It is to inform you that we have taken one more partner, Mr. Ramesh Shivram Gogate S/O shri. - B.S. Gogate in our partnership, with immediate effect.

From now, our company's current and savings accounts will be operated, namely, by

1. Kishore Joglekar

2. Ravindra Desai

3. Ramesh Shivram Gogate

A certified copy of our new partnership deed is enclosed for your information, record and necessary action. However, we shall call on you personally, in a couple of days, to sign the required papers/documents.

With thanks,

186. Requesting a Customers to Close His Account

Dear Sir,

I regret to inform you that a cheque for Rs. 1200/- drawn in your account has been returned unpaid today for lack of sufficient funds on your account.

For the last six months it has been necessary to return six cheques unpaid, for you had neglected to make provisions.

You will appreciate that it is bad for you and quite damaging to the reputation of the Bank.

I am, therefore, reluctantly compelled to request you to close your account.

187. To a Customer Seeking Advice on Investments

Dear Sir,

Please refer to your letter of -- December seeking advice for suitable investments.

I regret to say, as a matter of policy, the Bank does not venture to give advice on such matters. However in your case I forwarded your request to one of our brokers whose advice in the matter is enclosed.

I wish to point out that the information obtained is on your behalf and is being conveyed to you on a clear understanding that it does not involve any responsibility of the Bank or any of its officials.

188. To a Customer Seeking Advice on Purchase of Shares in Banks

Dear Sir,

I have the pleasure to refer to your letter of December -- 20-- seeking advice on your proposed purchase of shares in Banking companies and to inform you that the Bank does not undertake to advise its customers about their investments, as it will not like to involve itself in any liability.

However, I forwarded your request to our Brokers who feel that shares in the leading Banks are always a sound investment. They have recommended a representative selection showing as ready yield since you have specially emphasised a steady but remunerative return on the capital.

Their letter in original is enclosed, with a clear understanding that the advice tendered does not involve any liability of the Bank or any of its officials.

189. Acknowledging Instructions by a Customer

Dear Sirs,

We acknowledge receipt of your letter of December -- with your instructions to pay monthly school fees of your children and your quarterly life Insurance Premium on your behalf.

These instructions have been noted and will be complied with.

190. Request for Loan Without Security

Dear Sir,

In view of the approaching festive season, I am in urgent need of a loan of Rs. -- to purchase further fresh stocks. I have already taken good worth Rs. -- on credit from my suppliers. But they are unwilling to extend further credit facility and want cash payments.

This loan I want for a period of a month and a half. Last time you were good enough to grant me advance of Rs.-- for a period of 2 months in similar circumstances without any security, and I repaid it within the stipulated time.

I shall be obliged if you could again grant me a loan for the above amount and period. I shall be glad to call on you at your earliest convenience to discuss the matter with you personally.

191. Asking a Customer to Seek Overdraft Arrangements

Dear Sirs,

I would like to draw your attention to the fact that by payment today of a cheque of Rs. 1100 your account is overdrawn to the extent of Rs. 400.

I shall like to remind you that as a rule the Bank does not honour cheques drawn in excess of credit of an account, unless special arrangements have been made before hand for overdraft facilities by providing sufficient security.

Of course, in this instance, I did not hesitate to honour your cheque. But if you require to overdraw your account in future, you are advised to make proper arrangements with the Bank. By doing so, you will safeguard the risk of your cheques likely to be dishonoured for lack of sufficient funds to your credit.

192. To a Bank for Overdraft Facilities

Dear Sir,

We wish to have overdraft facility for which we are prepared to deposit with you bonds of Government Loans for Rs. 10,000. Will you please therefore, send us the necessary forms for signature? If further particulars are necessary, our manager will be glad to see you at any time convenient to you.

193. Reply to Above

Dear Sirs,

With reference to you letter dated -- March, 20--. we are enclosing the necessary forms and promissory notes for signature. After signing, please return them to us along with the bonds of Government Loans endorsed in our favour, on receipt of which we shall do the needful in the matter.

194. To a Customer Regretting Inability to Grant Overdrafts

Dear Sirs,

I have received your letter of -- December, 20-- applying for an overdraft of Rs. -- on the security of the deeds of the property in Rasta peth, Pune in the name of shri Vikas Patil.

I regret to inform you that the Bank is unable to accede to your request on account of insufficiency of the cover offered. The suggested security does not fully cover the risk. We can therefore, permit an overdraft of Rs. -- But if you can lodge with us an additional security, we shall reconsider your request for overdraft of a higher amount.

195. For Transfer of an Account to Another Branch

Dear Sir,

We enclose the completed form in respect of M/s Shubham Motors who will like their Current Deposit Account to be transferred to your Branch, as they have shifted to Nigadi.

Our relations have been quite cordial with them for the last two years of their account, and during the last two months they have been availing themselves of overdraft facilities of Rs. -- against the security lodged with us.

In due course, we shall forward you the deeds left with us as a security against the advance drawn by the firm.

196. Requesting Banker to Finance the Purchase of Car

Dear Sir,

Further to my personal meeting and discussion with you yesterday, on the matter noted above, I am enclosing the latest balance sheet of our firm, along with a photocopy of assessment for the year ending 31 March, 20--.

A cheque No. -- dated -- February, 20--, for Rs. -- is enclosed. Also find enclosed a set of your three forms in duplicate, duly filled in and signed by all the three partners of the firm.

Please issue a pay order for Rs. -- only is favour of M/s India, Thane Motors towards the full cost of a Maruti 800 car.

With thanks,

197. Applying for a Loan to a Bank

Dear Sir,

We are interested is getting a loan of Rs. -- against mortgaging our business property wroth Rs. --. We shall be glad to have your terms at your earliest. The loan is required for a period of 8 months.

198. Reply to Above

Dear Sirs,

We thank you for your letter dated -- November. 20--.

We shall be glad to give you a loan of Rs. -- against your property @ 12.5% per annum.

We are enclosing herewith necessary forms regarding mortgaging of property and request you to please return us the same after doing the needful.

Thanking you,

199. Request to Stop Payment of a Cheque

Dear Sir,

I hereby confirm my advice on telephone today in the morning, to stop the payment of a cheque detailed below:

Cheque No. -- dated -- February, 20-- for Rs. -- only, issued by me in favour of Safe Pack Ltd., Ballard Estate, Mumbai.

Please advise me soon of having done the needful in this respect.

With thanks,

200. Sending Documents through Bank

Dear Sir,

Please find the following documents enclosed :

1. Invoice No. -- dated -- April, 20--For Rs. --, and

2. R/R No. -- Dated -- April 20--

Please send these two documents to Unique components S.P. Road, Bengaluru against payment of Rs. 20,000/- (Rupees Twenty thousand only).

This payment, after collection, may be sent to us by a Demand Draft. In case these documents are not cleared within 16 days from today, please write to us immediately for further necessary instructions.

All your bank-charges are to be collected from M/s Unique components S.P. Road, Bengaluru.

With thanks,

201. Request to Bankers for Reference

Dear Sir,

M/s Poona Metals, Raviwar peth, have placed an order with us for goods worth Rs. -- on open account. They have given us the name of your bank as a reference.

Therefore, we would like you to inform us, in strict confidence, regarding their financial status and creditworthiness. Will it be safe to grant them credit facility for such a large amount now, and also in the future? We would particularly like to know how long they have had an account with you, and whether or not any of their debts are due for payment.

Once again, we may assure you that any information given to us in this matter would be regarded as secret and confidential.

A prepaid and self-addressed envelope is enclosed for your convenience.

With thanks,

202. To a Customer Whose Cheque has been Dishonoured through Oversight

Dear Sir,

I have your letter of January -- 20-- to acknowledge and to express my deep regret for the inconvenience caused to you as a result of dishonour of your cheque for Rs. --.

I have looked into the matter and discovered that the error has been caused by delayed entry of your cash deposit of Rs. -- made on December --. 20--.

I assure you that sufficient care will be taken in future to avoid such a lapse.

203. Returning a Dishonoured Cheque

Dear Sirs,

I enclose a cheque for Rs. -- drawn by Excel Products on Bank of Baroda, Mahalaxmi Road, Kolhapur, which has been returned unpaid for reasons stated thereon.

We have debited you with the amount.

204. About Dishonoured Cheque

Dear Sir,

M/s Deep Associates, IDC Area, Ambad, Nasik, have informed us that a cheque No. -- dt. -- July, 20--, for Rs. -- drawn and issued in their favour, and drawn on your bank, has bounced because you refused to honour. The bounced cheque is marked 'Refer to Drawer', which refers to insufficient amount of balance in our Current Account No. --. But there was sufficient balance, and then a cheque No. -- for Rs. -- drawn in our favour was deposited on -- July. Thus, the total amount in our account was many times over the amount of the dishonoured cheque.

This refusal of payment to the party against our cheque has caused us a lot of embarrassment, and loss of face. We wonder, how this has happened. Moreover, if there was any payment problem, at least you could have told us on phone.

We never expect such a lapse on the part of our bankers.

Please look into the matter soon, and inform us why this cheque was dishonoured.

205. Informing a Customer of Return of His Cheque

Dear Sirs,

I regret to inform you that your cheque No. -- in favour of M/s Rajlaxmi Printers for Rs. -- was presented for payment this day through Punjab National Bank and was returned unpaid for lack of funds in your account.

I shall urge the importance of retaining sufficient funds to meet your cheques or of arranging on overdraft against the deposit of satisfactory security.

The present balance in your account is Rs -- to your credit.

206. Returning Cheque

Dear Sirs,

We are returning here with Cheque No. .... dated ..... for Rs. ......
on ...... reason(s) gives on the Memo attached there to, viz. ....

Please note that your account has been debited with the amount of
the cheque.

207. Memo for a Cheque Returned Unpaid

Cheque Return Memo

For ....

Cheque No. .... Dated............ for Rs. .... drawn by ......
returned for reason(s) No. (s) ....

1. Refer to Drawer.
2. Not arranged for.
3. Full cover not received.
4. Drawer's signatures incomplete / differ / required.
5. Effects not cleared : Present again.
6. Payment stopped by drawer.
7. No advice.
8. Revenue stamp required.
9. Cheque bears extraneous matter.
10. ....
11. ....
12. ....

208. Requesting Bankers to Discount Bills

Dear Sir,

Please discount the enclosed bills and place their amount to our
credit.

Particular of Bills :

1. .....
2. ......
3. ....
4. Dated ....

Please acknowledge the receipt of this letter.

209. To Bankers about Non-Payment of Documents

Dear Sir,

The above documents were sent to you by registered post on -- April, 20--.

As per our instructions in the covering letter, the documents were returnable immediately after the lapse of 16 days, in case they remained uncleared by then. We presume that the documents have been released by M/s Rajat Enterprises, Business Centre, Camp, Pune and the amount of Rs. -- has been received by you from this party, besides your bank charges. But, we are sorry to state that so far, we have not received your draft for the above amount. Please sent it immediately.

If per chance the documents are still uncleared, they must be returned to us immediately.

We look forward to your early response and action in the matter. With thanks.

210. Informing a Customer of His Keeping Insufficient Funds

Dear Sir,

I would like to draw your attention to your Savings Bank Account No. -- which has not been properly maintained by you.

The amount to your credit has been below Rs. -- /- for the last six months.

You are advised to keep your accounts in order, failing which we shall request you kindly to close your account.

211. Requesting a Bank to Issue a Dollar Draft

Dear Sir,

This is to request you to please supply us a dollar draft for -- dollars in favour of Mercury Travels, Dadar, Mumbai, and debit the equivalent amount in rupee currency to our account.

212. Reply to Above

Dear Sirs,

With reference to your letter dated 14th July, we enclose the dollar draft for -- dollars. We have debited your account with Rs. --/- (Rs. -- per dollar plus Rs. -- as draft charges).

Thanking you,

213. Sending R/R through Bank

Dear Sir,

We are sending here with our invoice No. --- long with R/R No. - and request you to please realise the amount from the party concerned through the Canara Bank, Mumbai and credit the amount to our account on realisation. The bank charges will be paid by the party.

214. Sending R/R through Bank

Dear Sir,

We enclose here with :

1. R/R No .... dated ..... (freight paid).
2. Bill No. .... dated ...... for Rs. .....

and request you to please deliver the same to :

....

....

....

against payment of Rs....... (Rupees .... and paise ..... only).

The proceeds may the please be remitted to us by a Bank Draft marked 'Payee's A/C only' collecting all your charges from the party concerned.

Documents if uncleared within fifteen days may please be returned to us without any further instruction from this end.

215. Sending Documents through Bank

Dear Sir,

We enclose here with :

1. R/R No...... dated ..... (freight paid)
2. Bill No. ...... dated ...... for Rs. ......
3. Hundi for payment at 60 days's sight and request you to please deliver the same to :

....
....
....

Rs. ..... and Paise ...... only at 60 day's sight.

The proceeds may then please by remitted to us by a Bank Draft marked 'Payee's A/C only' collecting all your charges from the party concerned.

Documents if uncleared within seven days from the date of maturity may please be returned to us without any further instructions from this end.

216. To Bank Enquiring about Status of a Customer

Dear Sir,

May we please request you to favour us with your opinion as to the means and standing of the party whose name appears below. Please rest assured that any information you may favour us with will be treated as strictly private and confidential.

Name : Naveen Sharma
Designation : Partner.
Address : ....
....
Thanking you.

217. Reply to Above

Dear Sir,

With reference to your letter dated the --- August, we are enclosing the report as desired. Please note that the report is being sent in confidence and the bank will not accept any responsibility whatsoever. Futher, the name of this bank must not be disclosed in the event of passing on this report to anyone else.

218. Form of a Demand Hundi

Rs. .---------

On Demand please pay of New Bank of India Ltd. or order the sum of Rs. ------- (Rupees -------------------- being the net cost of three parcels sent by passenger train together with all charges for value received.

for Rex Cables

To,

      Ravindra Electricals
      100, feet Road
      Coimbtore

219. Form of a Sight Hundi

Sudharshan Electricals
M. G. Road,
Pune.
Dated ......

Rs. ---------

Forty five days after sight please pay to the Punjab National Bank or order the sum of Rs ------- (Rupees --------------------) together with all charges for value received against R/R G.P. 1605 enclosed.

for Sudarshan Electricals

To,

      Messrs. Krishna Power Products
      S. P. Road
      Bengaluru

220. Requesting Bankers to Send Pass Book

Dear Sir,

It is nearly four months since we opened a current account with you in the name of Sohan Computers. but we regret to bring it to your kind notice that we have not as yet received our pass-book.

As you know in the absence of bank pass-book, it is not possible for us to reconcile our accounts. We, therefore, request you to immediately look into the matter.

Thanking you,

221. Enclosing Cheque / Draft

Dear Sir,

We send you here with cheque / draft No. .... dated .... for Rs.

..... on ..... being the proceeds of your Bills No. ..... dated ...... in the name of .....

Please acknowledge the receipt.

222. Advising Bank for Treating the Issued Cheque as Cancelled

Dear Sir,

Our cheque No. ..... dated ..... issued in favour of Messrs. New Age Printers, for the sum of Rs. ..... /- seems to have been lost in transit. We request you to please treat the same as cancelled and do not pay as and when presented as we have today issued a fresh cheque for the same amount in favour of New Age Printers.

Thanking you,

223. Bank Informing a Customer that his Account has been Debited or Credited.

Dear Sirs,

The Manager presents his compliments and begs to advise that your ..... Accounts has been credited / debited with Rs. .... on account of ......

224. To a Customer Informing That His Current Account Has Been Overdrawn

Dear Sirs,

After encashing your cheque No. ...... dated .... for Rs. ..... issued in favour of Messrs. ...... your account has been overdrawn by Rs. ...... We, therefore, request you to please remit us this amount at your earliest convenience as our Current Acount Rules do not permit any such overdraft without previous arrangement with the Bank.

Thanking you,

225. Insurance of Goods against All Risks

Dear Sir,

Please insure the goods, mentioned as per list attached in the name of Messre. Tejpal & Co. The goods are to be insured against all risks.

Kindly let us know the amount payable to enable us to send you our cheque.

Thanking you,

226. Insurance of Goods Lying in Godown

Dear Sirs,

Please insure the goods against fire, as per details mentioned in the enclosed proposal form. Goods worth Rs. -- are lying in our godown at the above address.

227. Reply to Above

Dear Sirs,

We thank you for your letter dated – April along with your proposal form and have pleasure in informing you that the proposal has been accepted by this company. The policy is being prepared and will be sent to you in due course. Meanwhile we are sending our Cover Note giving the requisite cover.

Thanking you and assuring you of our best services,

228. Insurance Regarding Loss by Fire

Dear Sir,

We regret to inform you that a fire broke out in our godown located at the above address at about 11.00 p.m. last night. Watchman of the locality, who immediately contacted the fire brigade on phone. The fire brigade reached there at 11.30 p.m. but by that time the premises had been completely gutted, and it was only at 1.00 a. m. that the fire brigade was able to extinguish the fire successfully. The undersigned reached there at 11.30 p.m. having been informed on the incident by the watchman on phone.

We estimate a total loss of Rs. --/- and request you to please send you surveyor on Inspector to assess the loss and let us know what formalities are to be completed for putting up a claim for the loss.

229. Reply to Above

Dear Sirs,

With reference to your letter dated – November please be informed that our surveyor, Shri Manjeet singh, will call on you on -- December to assess the loss Meanwhile please fill in the attached form and return the same by first mail.

230. Enclosing Cheque for Settlement

Dear Sirs,

With further reference to you claim form and our surveyor's report we are sending herewith a cheque for --/- in full and final settlement.

Please send us you official receipt for the amount.

231. Request to Insure Goods Shipped - All Risks

Dear Sirs,

Please insure for an against all risks Rs. --/- value of ten cases of iron bars, marked : India Steel and shipped for account of Messrs. Excell steel Colombo, Shri Lanka by S.S. 'Manchester' sailing on 3rd October. Be good enough to effect this at once, and let us have the certificate by bearer, as we wish to forward it as early as possible.

232. Asking for Life Insurance

Dear Sir,

My wife, my son aged 15 years. and I am interested in getting ourselves insured for life.

Therefore, I would appreciate if you send your representative with necessary proposal forms etc., on any day during this fortnight, in the afternoon. Better if he fixes an appointment with me before visiting us. I may be contacted on telephone No....

Meanwhile, you may please send up some literature regarding life insurance in general, its advantages, and various schemes now in vogue, for our knowledge.

I look forward to an early response and visit by your agent.

Thanks,

233. Reply to Above

Dear Mr. Ramnath

Thank you for your letter of -- November, 20-- requesting us to send some literature, and our agent to help you in seeking life insurance for your wife, son and yourself.

We are glad to inform you that our agent, Mr. Manohar Rawale will call on you on Friday, -- November, 20-- at 2.30 P. M., to help you fill up the required proposal forms. He will also let you know in detail about the various life policies available with us, and their respective advantages.

Meanwhile, find enclosed some useful literature to help you have a general idea about life insurance and its different schemes/policies.

We look forward to provide you soon with the desired insurance for life.

With thanks,

234. Asking for Insurance Rates for a Consignment

Dear Sir,

We manufacture and sell exclusive gifts and novelty items in plastic, leather, rosewood and metal. These items are sent almost daily to different party of the country, in large packets worth Rs. -- to Rs. -- by road transport. We want your quotations to cover these goods against all risks while in transit from our factory to their destination.

Initially, we would like you to cover one consignment against all risks, from our place at the above address to Ahmedabad. The consignment is valued at Rs. -- and is to be transported by a local transport agency, next week.

We would, therefore, like you to send immediately, your rate for the cover of the above consignment.

235. Putting up Claim for Stolen Car

Dear Sir,

I am sorry to inform you that our Maruti -- Car No. -- insured with you against your Insurance Policy No. -- dated -- October, 20--, for Rs. -- was stolen from our office premises at the above address, during the night of August, 20--.

A complaint was lodged with the Sahakar Nagar Policy station the next morning vide FIR No. -- dated -- August 20--. A copy of it is enclosed for your reference.

In spite of the best efforts and lapse of so much time, the police have been unable to trace or recover the stolen car. Therefore, I am to request you to send me the insurance money for the car as soon as possible. I am enclosing the required claim forms in triplicate, duly filled in an signed.

I look forward to an early action and response in the matter.

With thanks,

236. Asking for the Surrender Value of a Life Policy

Dear Sir,

I have the above policy with you for Rs. -- and have been paying yearly premium of Rs. -- for the last 9 years. The due date of payment of premium is 8th December of every year.

Now, I am in urgent need of money and so would like you to let me know the surrender value of the policy including the bonus money accrued so far.

Please look into the matter immediately, and do the needful.

With thanks,

237. About Increase in Cover

Dear Sir,

I hold with you a Comprehensive Policy No. -- dated -- April 20-- for my car. The renewal of the policy is due next month. But now, I want to increase the amount of cover for my above car to Rs. -- from the present Rs. -- with effect from next month when the renewal of the above policy is due.

Therefore, please let me know the increase in premium, with the increase in the amount of cover of my car, from the next renewal date.

I look forward to your early response.

238. About Defective Insurance Policy

Dear Sir,

We thank you for your prompt despatch of our Policy No. -- dated August, 20-- against all risks of our consignment of Televisions for Rs. -- only, to be shipped to U.A.E. today. However, on the examination of the policy, we have noticed that you have not mentioned of "loss through pilferage and storm, cyclone and tornado."

If you go through the Proposal From to the above Insurance Policy, you will find this clause specially mentioned therein.

We are, therefore, returning the policy, and would appreciate your inserting the necessary words to cover loss through "Pilferage and storm, cyclone and tornado" as well.

With thanks,

239. To Insurance Co. Intimating Damage Done to the Goods and Asking for Compensation

Dear Sirs,

50 cases of white paper insured under Policy No. -- have been damaged en route from Mumbai to Pune owing to excessive rain.

As the goods are covered for this risk under policy referred to above, we request you to place reimburse us for Rs. --/- insured value of the goods. The goods lying in our godown and the necessary damage was shown to Transport Authorities who noted down in the records for any enquiry you might like to make form them.

Thanking you,

240. Reply to Above

Dear Sirs,

With reference to your letter dated the -- October, our Inspector, shri R. Pande will be visiting Pune on October.... Please render all possible assistance in assessing your claim.

Thanking you and assuring you of our best services,

241. Follow-up for Claim

Dear Sir,

With further reference to the inspection of damaged goods by your inspector, Mr. R. Pande on -- oct. we request you to expedite settlements of our claim for 50 cases of white paper.

Thanking you,

242. Final Settlement of Claim

Dear Sirs,

We acknowledge with thanks the receipt of your letter dated the -
- November.

We are enclosing herewith our cheque for 50 cases of white paper.
Please send us your official stamped receipt for the cheque.

Thanking you and assuring you of our best services,

243. The Proposer Submitting the Proposal of Insurance.

Dear Sir,

Enclosed please find duly filled in proposal from and a cheque
No. drawn on Union Bank of India, Mumbai for Rs. -- Kindly send the
cover note at the earliest.

244. Asking for the Surrender Value of a Policy

Dear Sirs,

Subject : Endowment Policy with benefits No. --

I have the above policy with you for Rs. --. And I have been paying
yearly premium of Rs. -- for the last 9 years.

Would you please let me know the surrender value of my policy
including the bonus money accrued so far as I am in urgent need of
money.

Please look into the matter immediately and do the needful.

245. From the Insured to the Insurance Company Informing about the Fire and the loss to the Building and the Stock

Dear Sir,

We regret to inform you that our factory premises, insured with
you, and situated at 73, Industrial Area, Bhosari, Pune caught fire on
October 20-- at 2.30 a. m. due to short circuit. We immediately informed
the Fire Brigade and the local police station about the incident.

There has been extensive damage to the factory building while the stock lying in there has been completely destroyed.

The damage to the building is estimated to Rs. -- lakh, while loss to stock has been to the extent of Rs. --.

Kindly send a claim form and instruct your inspectors or surveyors to assess the loss at the earliest.

246. Notice of Board Meeting

Dear Sirs,

The next meeting of the Directors will be held at the registered office of the Company on Saturday, the --th November, at 4 p. m. When the business mentioned in the enclosed agenda will be considered.

247. Sending Minutes of the Board Meeting to a Member

Dear Sir,

I am forwarding herewith a copy of the minutes of the Board's Meeting held on November, 20--.

Your attention is particularly drawn to item No. -- and --.

248. Notice to the Shareholders of an Annual General Meeting

Dear Sir,

Notice is hereby given that the Seventeenth Ordinary General Meeting of the Shareholders of the above Company will be held at the registered office of the Company on Monday, the -- June, 4 p. m. to transact the following :

1. To announce the audited accounts including balance sheet for the period from 1st April, - to 31st March.
2. To appoint a Director in place of Shri Raunak Dosi who died last month.
3. To approve auditors for the current year and to fix their fees.
4. To declare dividend.

The share Transfer Books of the Company will be closed from the -- June to -- June.

You are requested to attend the above meeting.

249. Application for the Transfer of Shares

Dear Sir,

Please transfer shares Nos. -- to -- in the name of Shri .... to my name.

Thanking you,

250. Informing a Shareholder That His Share have been Lodged for Transfer

Dear Sir,

This is to inform you that an instrument of transfer purporting to be signed by you and transferring 20 shares, numbered -- to -- (both the numbers inclusive) of the Company, now standing in your name, has been lodged at this office for registration.

In case we do not hear from you to the contrary within seven days from the date of this letter, we will presume that the matter is in order and we will deal with the instrument of transfer in the usual manner.

251. From a Shareholder Enquiring about the Company's Progress and the Likelihood of a Higher Dividend

Dear Sir,

I am a shareholder of your Company for the last fifteen years and I have got as many as -- ordinary shares. I have been offered -- shares at a premium of 5% and I shall feel much obliged if you would kindly let me know the progress being made by the company and the likelihood of any increase in the dividend in the near future.

252. Reply to Above

Dear Sir,

Thank you for your letter dated -- April.

I regret, in the capacity of a Secretary, I am unable to give you the information. I am sure you will appreciate my position as in giving you any such information, I should be acting in a manner prejudicial to the interest of other shareholders.

However, I suggest you to go through the latest Director's Report and the Balance Sheet and consult your stock brokers who may be in a position to help you.

253. To the Registrar of Companies, Accompanying Audited Balance Sheet, etc.

Dear Sir,

In compliance with section .... of the Indian Companies Act we beg to send herewith for filing the Annual List of Members and Summary duly signed, together with the necessary certificates and three copies of the audited Balance Sheet and Profit and Loss Account for the year ending -- December, --, adopted at 4th Ordinary General Meeting of the Shareholders of the Company held on March, 20 --

Rs. ...... being the requisite amount of filing fees is sent herewith.

254. To Share-Holders Proposing Amalgamation

Dear Sir / Madam,

In pursuance of the policy laid down at the last General Meeting, the Directors have finalised the details for the amalgamation of interests of this Company with Goa Films Ltd. Goa.

The Directors are fully convinced that Goa Films Ltd. Goa enjoys a good financial standing and has sufficient dividend earning capacity.

The amalgamation will strengthen the company and ensure it against a sterner competition.

The basis of the proposed amalgamation agreed upon by the Board of the two Companies will be exchange of one ordinary share in J.P. Films Ltd. for one ordinary share in Goa Films Ltd.

It is hoped, you will formally support the resolution authorising the exchange of shares.

255. To a Shareholder Who Claims Higher Dividend in the Light of the Profits

Dear Sir,

I am directed to inform you that the Board had given a careful attention to the points raised by you in your letter of August -- before recommending the declaration of a dividend of -- percent. Before arriving at this decision, the Board had borne in mind the financial strength of Company and the general conditions of trade.

In the candid opining of the Board, higher dividend was not justified in the larger interest of the Company.

256. To Bankers for Overdraft

Dear Sir,

I have been directed by the Board of Directors to enquire whether the Bank will allow the Company an overdraft not exceeding Rs. two lakhs for a period of 5 months.

The overdraft is required to finance a valuable contract that the Company has secured for supply of vehicles to the Pune Municipal Corp.

The Directors suggest a floating charge over the company's assent and undertaking as security for the overdraft. The Board will, accordingly, pass a Resolution authorising the borrowing and the creation and the execution of the charge.

I am enclosing a copy of the company's Balance sheet, and I shall be glad to furnish you with any information that you may like to seek.

257. To Bankers Refusing to Recognise Notice of a Lien on Shares

Dear Sir,

Reference your letter No. -- dated -- purporting to be a notice of the deposit of certain certificates of shares in the Company.

I am directed to inform you that the Company is unable to recognise or to take any action upon the said letter, which is returned herewith.

258. By a Newly Incorporated Company to Open an Account in a Bank

Dear Sir,

It has been decided in the meeting of the board to open a current account of the company in your bank. Necessary documents, listed below, are enclosed :

1. Copy of the Memorandum of Association.
2. Copy of the Articles of Association.

3. Copy of the Certificate of Incorporation and "Certificate of Commencement of Business."
4. A certified copy of Resolution No. -- passed by Board of Directors of January -- 20-- authorising the opening of a bank account.
5. The application form duly filled in for opening the bank account.
6. Specimen signatures of the Chairman and the Secretary of the Company who will operate the account.
7. Rs. -- in cash and a pay-in-slip for depositing Rs. --.

Please open the current account in the name of the company and send to me a cheque book containing -- cheques, the pass book and pay-in-slip book with the counter foil of the pay-in-slip for Rs. --

259. For Opening Company's Account in Bank

Dear Sir,

We wish to open a current account in the name of our company as decided by the Board of Directors in the Resolution enclosed.

Please send us the requisite forms, alongwith necessary instructions. We shall be pleased to know what facilities you will be able to offer to the company.

260. To a Shareholder Removing His Doubts

Dear Sir,

I am directed to refer of your letter of December -- and to inform you that all the rumours for the absorption of this Company in some other company are ill-founded and malicious.

We are rather surprised to know what led to this speculation.

With kind regards,

261. To Shareholders for Reconstructing the Company

Dear Sir/Madam,

I am directed to enclose Notice of an Extraordinary General Meeting of the Company to be held at Grand Hotel Mumbai on Monday, -- February 20-- at 10 a. m.

The meeting has been convened to consider a reconstruction scheme for the development of the Company's property.

The Directors are convinced that the proposed scheme will fully safeguard the interests of the share-holders.

A form of proxy in enclosed which may please be sent back, duly signed.

262. To Shareholders Intimating Bonus Shares

Dear Sir/Madam

I am directed to inform you that Board of Directors have decided to issue bonus shares.

An outline of the scheme has been drafted and is enclosed for your information. This will come up for consideration and final approval in the meeting of the General Body which will be held on January -- 20-

I trust, you will support the proposed scheme which is being introduced to further the interests of the company.

263. Inviting to Join the Board of a Company

Dear Sir,

I am directed by the Board of Directors to extend a cordial invitation to you to join the Board of the Company. The Directors feel that your vast experience and foresight will be a great asset, besides the honour that your association will bestow upon the Company.

The Chairman will be pleased to discuss the matter with you personally and explain the financial and commercial status of the company.

A copy each of the Company's Memorandum and Articles of Association is enclosed, together with the latest published Balance Sheet.

264. To Solicitors for Stopping Infringement of a Patent

Dear Sirs,

It has been brought to notice of the company that an infringement of our Patent No ...... for Iron and Steel Forging has been committed by Western steel Forgings, Mumbai.

We wish to seek redress through a court of law and claim damages for the loss suffered by us.

Relevant documents are enclosed for your perusal and suitable remedial measures in matter.

265. To Solicitors Enclosing Documents

Dear Sirs,

I enclose for your attention the following documents, as desired by you :

1. Our notice to Western Steel Forgings.
2. Reply from Western Steel Forgings to our notice.
3. Photostat copy of our Patent.

We shall be glad to send you any other material that you may require.

266. To Solicitors for Drafting the Resolution

Dear Sirs,

At a meeting of the Board of Directors held on December -- a Resolution was passed for calling an extraordinary general meeting of the company to sanction an increase of capital and captalisation of reserves.

I have been accordingly directed to ask you to draft the necessary Notice and Resolution.

Following documents are enclosed for your perusal.

1. A copy of the Resolution passed by the Board.
2. A copy each of the Memorandum and Articles of Association.
3. Balance Sheet.

267. To a Property Dealer Requesting Him to Find Out a Suitable Accommodation

Dear Sir,

We shall be glad if you can render us assistance to find out suitable accommodation for the Bank.

The present premises are not large enough to accommodate the staff which greatly hampers the smooth functioning of the Branch.

We shall require two big halls measuring around -- ft. by -- ft. and -- ft. -- ft. We shall prefer to have spacious uncovered verandah outside on the ground floor. We shall be able to pay upto a rent of Rs. --/- p. m. with one year's rent in advance.

268. From a Property Dealer for Offer of Property

Dear Sir,

Since your enquiry last week, for a suitable house, we have been looking for a house to suit your requirements. We are pleased to bring to your notice a good house Link Road, Bandra (west)

The house is quite spacious with five bed rooms (bath attached), garage and servant's out house, The price demanded is Rs. -- lakhs.

We must say it is an ideal property, and for the price asked for it appears to be a good bargain.

We have some other parties too, who are interested in similar properties, but we have made you the first offer.

Kindly make up your mind and visit us to see the house.

Assuring you of the best of our attention.

269. For Taking over Premises on Lease

Dear Sir,

As you are aware, I am very much interested in taking over from you your existing lease in regard to the above premises. My representative called on you a few days back and inspected the premises, and discussed the matter with you in detail, and now I feel quite satisfied.

Meanwhile, would you please send me a copy of the lease deed so that I may consult my lawyer. I want that both of us meet in the near future on a mutually convenient date to decide the issue of premium etc.

I look forward to your immediate response.

270. To a Property Dealer for Office Premises

Dear Sir,

Following our man's short visit to your office last Monday. I want to inform you that we require office space either in Model colony or Gokhale Nagar and nowhere else. We want office accommodation with approximately -- sq. ft. floor area with W. C. and a kitchenette. It should also have telephone and fax facilities.

Rent is no constraint, but we want excellent location and all modern facilities. As far as decoration and furnishing is concerned, we would get it done ourselves to our liking.

This office space is required for a long duration, say for -- years, but initially it may be on lease for a short period of -- years, renewable further for longer durations.

On hearing from you, I would come over there personally and settle the issue after due formalities. We may again underline it that we need the office space urgently.

271. Reply to Above

Dear Shri Subodh,

Thank you for your letter of -- August regarding office space in Model Colony or Gokhale Nagar. We have 3-4 excellent offers to suit your specific requirement. These office premises have all the facilities you have asked for including fax, telephone, kitchenette and western style W. C. Moreover, they are well and tastefully furnished, and perhaps you would be fully satisfied after having a look at these and then change your mind as for as redecorating is concerned.

The space available in Model Colony is on the first floor, but really excellent. The other two are in Gokhale Nagar and on the ground floor. Both are equally good and have prime location. But you must be quite quick in the matter as there are a few other parties who are really very much interested to have these for their office.

I look forward to your immediate response and action in the matter. With thanks,

272. Offering a Godown

Dear Sir,

I have since discussed the matter with the owner of the godown which has been recently constructed. It is -- sq. mt. in area, and the major portion of it is covered while the rest of it is open. In front of it there is a huge parking space for trucks, lorries etc. Moreover, it is on main Road, and, therefore suits well to your requirements.

The owner is willing to give it on lease, initially for the period of 3 years only, on monthly rent of Rs. -- and a security deposit of Rs. -- only. This lease can be renewed for a further period of 3-4 years with the condition that there is suitable increase in rent at the time of renewal.

The rent and security are to be paid strictly by cheques. He also insists that 3 month rent should be paid in advance. You will have to pay for water and electricity charges, besides Municipal tax.

In my opinion it is an excellent offer and you should accept it immediately lest some other party grabs the offer. Send immediately your representative to inspect the premises and to discuss the matter in detail so that the lease deed may be finalised and payments made in the near future.

Thanks,

273. Reply to Above

Dear Mr. Sharma,

Thank you for your letter of -- April regarding availability of a Godown on main road. The details of the godown and the terms and conditions of the landlord suit us and we would at once like to strike the deal.

Our Company Secretary, along with the Assistant Accountant, would call on you on -- May in the afternoon. He is fully authorised to discuss and negotiate the deal. He will also issue the cheques for the required amounts. Meanwhile, you please get the draft of the lease ready, which may be executed immediately after the deal. We want to have the possession of the godown latest by -- of May 20--

274. For Showroon-cum-Office Space on Rent

Dear Sir,

It is in response to your advertisement in a couple of national dailies of today regarding availability of 900 sq. feet of space for showroom-cum-office in Bhikaji Cama Place, Main plaza, Upper Ground Floor, Near Ring Road. We find the advertisement interesting, and the space suitable for opening our showroom there.

We manufacture Notebook Computers and Laser and Dot matrix Printers in collaboration with a famous foreign giant in this field. We want to open our showroon in Bhikaji Cama Place and so, find your advertisement interesting. But we would like you to send us more details about the space available. We would like to purchase the showroom-cum-office space outright if the owner is willing. If not, we may take it on lease.

We would furnish it ourselves according to our taste and needs, but hope telephone and fax facilities already exist there. However, we would manage all these if they are not already there. Rent and Security money etc. are no constraints. What we want is excellent prime location to suit our purpose of a showroom.

Please send the full details soon so that we may proceed further in the matter.

275. Requesting for Renewal of Lease

Dear Mr. Dayal,

We may remind you well in time that the lease of the above office premises expires on -- July, 20-- as per the terms and conditions of the lease deed. We want to continue our business activities from this place, and so request you to extend the lease for a further period of 3 years with effect from -- August, 20-- on the same terms and conditions. However, we are willing to increase the present rent by 18% in view of the high maintenance costs and inflated property tax. We hope this increase in monthly rent would satisfy you.

We look forward to an early response so that a lease agreement can be executed in time before the lapse of the present one. Our representative would call on you some time next week to discuss the matter, and to tell you what urgent repairs are to be done at the premises.

276. Remitting Rent

Dear Sir,

We have pleasure in enclosing, in advance, a bunch of 5 post-dated cheques, Nos. -- to -- for Rs. -- each, drawn on syndicate Bank, Laxmi Road branch.

These 5 post-dated cheques are towards rent for the months of may to September, 20--.

Please acknowledge the receipt of these cheques by signing and returning the attached voucher for our record and future reference.

Thanks,

---

277. Asking for Estimate for Decoration of Office Premises

Dear Sir,

I would like to get our office space measuring -- sq. feet on the Ground Floor renovated, refurnished and decorated. I want to have a complete new look in respect of furniture, backdrop cabinets, carpet and well-painting.

Therefore, please send your Architect and Designer at the earliest with quotations, samples etc. so that the matter can be discussed in detail and orders given.

I want time-bound, guaranteed work within the shortest time possible, so that our work does not suffer. Please let me know by return of post when your man is coming. I hope you can appreciate the urgency of the matter. In case I don't receive immediate response, I am likely to entrust the work to some other competent party. I am actually interested in giving you this job because one of my very intimate friends and business-fellows has recommended your name.

I look forward to your immediate response.

278. To a Property and Estate Agent for Residential Accommodation for Company's Managing Director

Dear Sir,

We are in urgent need of a suitable residential accommodation for our Managing Director. The independent self-contained and furnished dwelling unit should be on the ground floor, preferably in Shivaji Nagar Or Model Colony with front lawn and servants quarter.

This accommodation for residential purpose is required on lease for long term, which may be initially for a period of three years, but further renewable for longer durations.

We may underline the fact that rent etc. are no constraint for us but we want a well-furnished bungalow with a lot of open space and lawn around. Garage and servants quarter are a must.

Please send your offer/proposal soon with full details, either by post or by your representative, to our Addl. Director (Finance), Mr. Raj Saxena.

279. Announcement of New Sole Agents

Dear Mr. Smith

We feel pleasure in announcing that we have non appointed Messrs. Tarang Distributors to act as our sole agents and stockists in Chennai for all our products.

We thank you for your confidence reposed in us and for orders sent to us in the past. Now we request you to order your requirements in future through our sole agents in the city.

They will have all our products in large and sufficient quantity and numbers to deliver quickly all your future requirements. Meanwhile, we shall continue, as usual, to send you our catalogues, pamphlets and price lists regarding our old and new products from time to time.

We want to assure you that our present standards of service and delivery will be well maintained through our sole agents.

280. Circular about Change of Address

Dear Sir/Madam,

To serve all our valuable customers more efficiently and promptly, we have moved to this new place at 315, Vithalwadi, Sinhgad Road, Pune - 411051. Consequently, our Telephone, Telex and Fax numbers have also changed as noted above.

This is a far more spacious, centrally located, and conveniently approachable place, and it will go a long way to make your service more personalized and result-oriented. Please, from now on, send all your orders, enquiries, replies etc. to this new address, or pay us an early visit to see for yourself how we have arranged things to render you better personalised service.

With thanks,

281. Circular About Change in Company's Status

Dear Sir,

We are pleased to inform you that our company has been registered as a Private Limited Company with effect from -- Oct., 20--

Henceforth, you are required to address all your correspondence, orders, bills, enquiries, cheques, drafts etc. in favour of Merina Impex

Private Limited, at the address mentioned above.

Thanks for your valuable and continued co-operation and confidence in us.

282. Circular about Termination of Services of Sales Representative

Dear Sir,

Our Sales Representative, Mr. Rohan Kale is no more with us, as he has resigned and joined some other pharmaceutical company with effect from -- July, 20--.

Therefore, Mr. Kale is no more authorised to book orders for our products, collect payments, or make any kind of negotiations, commitments on our behalf. Anyone dealing with him will do so at his/her own risk and responsibility.

283. Announcing a New Publication

Dear Sirs,

We have pleasure in informing you that our first book Objective English is now out in the market.

Printed in nice white paper with -- pages, the book is priced at Rs. -- only.

It has been edited by Shri. Ravi Pathak - compiler of Perfect Essay- a book which has fetched tremendous sale during the last few months. We have already received quite a large number of bulk orders and find that the book is getting a very good sale. We are sending separately under book post a title of the book which speaks for itself.

Our terms of sale are :

Discount :   1 to 50 copies 25% F.O.R.

51 to 100 copies 35% F.O.R.

284. Announcing the Admission of a Partner

Dear Sirs,

I have pleasure in informing you that owing to the large increases in my business I have this day taken into partnership Shri Sukhram and that this business will henceforth be known under the style of :

Sukhsagar

Shri. Sukhram had been my Manager for the last ten years and has got adequate experience in this trade. Before joining me he had taken three years practical training in one of the world's leading lens manufacturing firms in Germany and has always taken keen interest in watching the latest and most modern methods of lens manufacturing.

Shri. Sukhram also brings a cash investment of Rs. -- and I hope we shall now be able to expand our business to the extent of marketing our products in areas which remained untouched owing to restricted production.

We are grateful to you for your patronage and we sincerely hope for a continuance of the same.

I remain,

285. Death of a Partner-Taking New Partner into Partnership

Dear Sirs,

I regret to announce the premature death of my much esteemed partner Mr. Anand Pant who was one of the founders of our firm and who was responsible for bringing this firm to its present position.

I have, however, pleasure in informing you that I have taken Shri. Rakesh Joshi the eldest son of Shri Narain Joshi into partnership. Shri. Rakesh Joshi had been working as a foreman for the last eight years and is fully familiar with the practical know-how of this trade. Besides, it was with his suggestion that we were able to increase our production capacity by 10% with the available source in our firm. We shall continue to trade under the same style and in exactly the same lines as before.

We thank you and feel proud of your past co-operation and we hope to receive the same in future also.

286. Retiring from Business

Dear Sirs,

I regret to inform you that I am retiring from business from the -- November and as I am now getting on in years I have decided to spend at least party of the autumn of life in the quite of my native village.

I have disposed of all my machinery to Messrs. Rajesh and Co., who have also taken part of my ready and raw stock. But some raw and manufactured stock is still with me which I want to dispose of by lots on cash. Since you have been one of my very good customers for the last twenty years and hence you have got good demand for my products, I suggest that you should make me an offer for the particular quantities suitable for your requirements.

I will always remember with feeling of pleasure the friendly relations we had for the last so many years and I sincerely wish you a continued and increasing prosperity.

I remain,

287. Announcing Conversion of a Partnership Firm into a Limited Company

Dear Sirs,

We are thankful to you and to all our customers whose continued patronage has brought our business position to our present stage. Of late our business requirements have increased to such an extent that our available capital is not sufficient in meeting demands of our customers. We have, therefore, decided to convert our firm into a private limited company which will come into existence from the -- of this month, and will be titled as :

Magna Infrastructure Pvt. Ltd.

With more capital, which will be forthcoming, we shall be able to expand our business and render much better service than we had been doing in the past. We assure you that the relation we have built with you during the past few years will be maintained as it is and our traditions built up will be upheld by the country.

We thank you once again and hope for your continued patronage as in the past.

288. Report on Shortage in Store

Dear Sirs,

I wish to bring to the notice of the Board of Directors the stock shortage that I have observed in my surprise check in the light of the general policy laid down by the directors.

There is a great deficiency in stock as recorder by storekeeper against the actual stock in hand. Some of the entries appear to have been cooked, which is evident from the fact that certain articles are found to be more in stock than on record.

This appears to be a clear case of deliberate wangling which has to be curbed to protect the interest of the company.

I, therefore, seek the instructions of the Board to proceed further in the matter.

289. Report on Desirability of Opening a Branch Abroad

Commissioned by the Board of Directors to visit Paris and report on the feasibility of opening a Branch there, I have following observations to make :

1. There is a great market of ready-made garments in France which is a land of beauty and fashion.
2. To maintain a regular link with the markets of France, a Branch of the Company at Paris will render a very useful service.
3. The Branch at Paris can also look after our trade interests in other European Countries.
4. Our competitors have already set up their Branches in the Capitals of most of the leading European Countries, and they are having a flourishing business.
5. Of all the Capitals of European countries, Paris can give us the maximum business.

290. Report on Indiscipline and Indifference of the Staff

I desire to bring to the notice of the Board of Directors a general state of apathy on the part of the senior officials of the company.

They are most unpunctual and irregular and above all they are not amenable to discipline. They seem to have started a regular move of lack of cooperation. Consequently, efficiency is on the decline, and I am afraid it will have its sad reflection on the business of the company.

If the Directors approve, a warning may be issued to the erring officials.

291. Report on Cash Shortage and Other Irregularities

Dear Sir,

As directed by the Directors, I have looked into periodical cash shortage and other irregularities in the cash branch. Inquiries have revealed that cash shortage is largely caused by the inefficiency of the cashier. His mode of work is unmethodical and he leaves much to memory. He shirks work and makes all the entries of the day at one time.

I therefore, strongly feel that he must be immediately replaced by a more conscientious worker.

Laxity in discipline is another snag. I am convinced that unless the company takes a strict view a breach of discipline despite the pressures of the Labour Unions, things will not improve.

292. Report Refuting Charges of Slackness

Dear Sir,

I have carefully looked into your observation on the slackness of the staff, but fail to find any substantial evidence of slackness on the part of any member of the staff.

I am enclosing a detailed monthly report of work done by all the members of the staff, which amply bears a testimony to the fact that all the employees of the company are most devoted loyal and conscientious workers.

I do not think it will be fair to reprimand them without any evidence of concrete lapse of omission and commission on their part.

I shall however, keep a through watch on their work and conduct, and I assure you that I shall not relent to take a suitable disciplinary action whenever there is cause for complaint.

293. Report on Threatened Strike by Workers

Dear Sirs,

I have to point out that the Labour Union have served a notice of strike, with effect from -- January 20--.... consequent on the refusal of the Board to concede to the demands for increase in the wages of the workers.

The attitude of the Union leaders smacks of lack of understanding and cooperation. Although the strike is not likely to last for a long time in view of the division in the union, yet I have taken necessary safeguards against all eventualities, including violence.

I would like to know if the Board will like to meet again to consider the threat of strike or the Company should adopt the wait-and see policy.

294. Committee's Report on Extension of Work

Indian Fashion Ltd.

Committee on Extension of work

The committee has after deliberations arrived at the following conclusions :

1. The company may set up its own units of designing, tailoring and outfitting which will ensure economy and better business.
2. This will enable the company to provide novelties and new attractions and thereby catch up more business.
3. All leading competitors of the company have their own units of weaving, manufacturing, designing, tailoring and outfitting to make a compact business.
4. The Company may set up its own Export Department to exclusively look to export business which has been on the increase, despite the haphazard and ill-planned export business undertaken by the company.
5. The Company may undertake marketing of allied goods which may be initially purchased from the local markets.

295. Committee's Report on Financial Position of the Company

Rajkumar Sons

Committee on Review of Financial Position.

Appointed by the Directors, the Committee has looked into the financial position of the Company and has following report to submit :-

Facts of the Case

1. The company is over-staffed and the distribution of work among the staff is irrational.
2. The company have been taking 20 type writers, 2 duplicating

machines and 30 ceiling fans on hire which involves a recurring expenditure of a very high order.

3. There is little follow - up programme to realise the outstanding debts of the company with the result that the circulation of money is hampered.

4. The trade discount offered by the company is 5% higher than that offered by the competitors.

5. The entertainment bills are inflated.

6. The company is housed in a very large building at a very high rent.

The Committee has, therefore, following recommendations to make :

1. Economy cut may be exercised in the staff by 20% and the work load may be more rationally distributed among the members of staff.

2. The equipment on hire may be purchased to reduce the high recurring expenditure bill.

3. Vigorous drive may be lunched to pursue old debts.

4. The trade discount offered may be made at par with the competitors.

5. Austerity may be ensured for one or two years.

6. The company may rent a cheaper accommodation.

7. Checks and counter checks may be adopted to tone up general efficiency.

296. Committee's Report on New Business Opening

Ram and Co. Ltd.

Sales Committee on New Business Openings

Appointed by the Board of Directors, the sales committee has conducted intensive survey to explore new openings for the business of the company.

Following are the deliberations of Committee :

1. The Company has comparatively no business in Punjab, Haryana, H. P., Delhi and Chandigarh which does not seem to have been explored, A Sales Representative may be appointed for this Zone, with his Head-quarters at Chandigarh.

2. The over-all publicity of the products of the Company is very

negligible which may be intensified to focus the attention of the buyers.

3. Exhibitions may be held at Bombay, Madras, Calcutta, Delhi and Chandigarh to create public interest in the products of the Company.
4. Season's discount may be offered to fetch more business.
5. Follow up correspondence may be arranged to boost up sales.

297. Report to Share-Holders on Offer for Purchase of Company

Dear Sir / Madam,

I am directed by the Directors to inform you that an offer has been received from M/s Raviraj Group for the purchase of the assets and the business of your Company, subject to the following terms and conditions:

1. The purchasers will take over the assets and liabilities with a status-quo of the staff who will be merged in their existing establishments.
2. The purchasers will increase the capital so, as to compete in a big way.
3. The purchasers will pay for the expenses of the winding up and make a cash payment of Rs. -- which will permit a distribution of Rs. -- is cash in respect of each share held by you.

The Directors feel that while your interests will be fully protected, the purchasers who possess most up-to-date plant and machinery and have a capacity to raise more capital will ensure a good business of the company. They, accordingly, recommend the acceptance of the offer.

A notice of an extra-ordinary general meeting to discuss this matter is enclosed.

298. Committee's Reports on Reorganisation of Office

Facts of the Case

The Committee has observed as under :

1. The Committee finds surplus staff in the Accounts Department, while the Administrative Department is understaffed.
2. The positions of Secretary and General Manager have been

combined in one incumbent who has only one assistant working under him.

3. The staff in the Correspondence Department are not well qualified. They are fit to work only as Junior Clerks.

4. Red tape exists in the disposal of work, resulting in unnecessary flow of paper boats.

Recommendations :

The Committee has following recommendations to make :

1. The General Duty Clerks, one Analyst one Typist of the Accounts Department may be drafted to the Administrative Department.

2. A separate full-time post of General Manager may be created with one assistant attached to him. The Secretary and General Manager may have separate full-time Stenographers attached to them.

3. Three posts of Sr. Assistants may be created in the correspondence Department who may work independently.

4. Unnecessary channels for disposal of work may be eliminated.

299. Report by Chartered Accountants

Dear Sirs,

In accordance with the instructions of your Managing Director we have examined the functioning of your staff and have arrived at the following :

1. There is red-tape in your office, and every official avoids doing things on his own intiative.

2. The accounts are haphazardly maintained, and there is no follow-up of the debts which have been allowed to pile up.

3. The Manager does not inspire respect of his staff, with the result that his instructions go unheeded.

4. Most of the members of the staff are of an inferior mettle.

We, therefore, feel that immediate steps must be taken to reorganise the company and stream line its working by bringing in one or two more experienced hands to man the responsibility and ensuring strict disciplinary action against defaulters.

300. Report on Heavy Book Debts

Dear Sir,

In accordance with your instructions given to me in the last meeting of the Board, I have looked in to the cause of heavy accumulation of debts of the company and come to the conclusion that most of our customers are hard-pressed as a result of increase in the cost of living, though they are good pay-masters. I have no doubt in my mind that rise in the debts can be attributed to general conditions of economic hardships of the class of customers we have, and it is not the result of any defective policy of the company.

I have personally met a number of customers, including foreign travellers, and I am led to believe that any curtailment in the credit facilities will give a serious set-back to the business of the company. It cannot be denied that our competitors are offering no less liberal terms of credit.

However, I am convinced that the difficulties of our customers are of a short duration which should not warrant any room for pessimism.

301. Report on a Fall of Business

Dear Sir,

As directed, I have made a through investigation to find out where the causes of decline in the company's business lie.

Facts of the Case

1. There has been virtually no new arrivals in the varieties we deal in.
2. Competitors have started selling goods at throw away prices.
3. Neglect of publicity on modern lines.
4. The general behaviour of the sales assistants is far from satisfactory.

Suggestions

1. More uniform lists of prices should be drawn to view with those of the competitors.
2. Streamlining the staff by appointing smart and business like representatives as Sales Assistants.

3. Planned publicity campaign to popularise our goods.

4. Maintenance of follow up correspondence with the old customers.

302. Report on an Accident

Dear Sirs,

I regret to report that on December -- at 5 p. m. the outer wall and a portion of the roof of the premises, owned and occupied by the company, collapsed all of a sudden, resulting in the killing of two daily-wagers who were on the work.

The collapse was quite unexpected, since it was checked up thoroughly about two months ago at the time of redecoration of the building. The architect, who was summoned immediately after the collapse, attributes it to two decayed beams and excessive vibrations which the weak walls were not able to sustain.

Of course, it is a great tragedy, but fortunately it is fully covered by insurance for the material and human loss. I have, accordingly, informed the Insurance Company, and submitted a formal claim.

The Managing Director has announced all assistance to the families of the victims, and he is calling a meeting of the Board (copy enclosed) to obtain confirmation of his action and decide on the further course of action.

303. Report on Insufficiency and Inadequacy of Accommodation

Dear Sirs,

The present premises of the Company are so inadequate that it has resulted in congestion consequent on the increase in the strength of the staff to 35 persons as a result of expansion of the Account Department.

Although some adjustments have been made by reducing the size of the office tables, yet the building is hardly sufficient even for the marginal adjustments.

I, therefore, seek to impress on the Directors the need for a more commodious accommodation in the interest of efficiency.

I shall be glad to receive your approval for renting a more suitable accommodation.

304. Application for the Post of Translation Officer

Dear Sirs,

With 7 years long experience and requisite qualifications as a Senior Translator/Interpreter, I have been looking for a change of job that would improve my prospects and status. And now, year advertisement in the Hindustan Times of -- August, 20-- for the post of Translation Officer offers me an opportunity.

My particulars regarding qualification, work experience, present post held etc. are given in the enclosed curriculum vitae.

I would very much appreciate your giving me an early opportunity to discuss the matter in detail, in person, at the time of interview.

With thanks,

CURRICULUM VITAE

1. Name : --
2. Address : --
3. Date of birth and age : --
4. Nationality : --
5. Marital Status : --
6. Educational Qualifications :
   (a) ....
   (b) ....
   (c) ....
   (d) ....
   (e) ....
7. Details of employment and experience

Company/Institution	Post Held	Form-To	Nature of Work
-	-	-	-
-	-	-	-
-	-	-	-

Present Post held :

Senior Translator as mentioned above. I have also translated 2 technical books relating to Electronics and Computer Science from Russian into English.

305. Application for the Post of Retail Manager

Dear Sir,

With reference to your advertisement in the Indian Express of -- April, 20-- for the post of a Retail Manager, I beg to offer myself as a candidate, as I am sure I possess all the necessary qualifications and experience, and desired expertise for the job.

I am a Commerce Graduate from Indira Gandhi Open University with first class and distinction in salesmanship and Book-keeping. I am really smart, polished and fluent in English, Hindi and I have been working for the last 3 years with a highly reputable company, and am posted in one of their showrooms here in a prestigious shopping complex.

My present employers are fully satisfied with my work and conduct. I have been instrumental in boosting their sales by more than 50% during the last one year because of my excellent communication and selling skills. Hence, I was given three advance increments. But now I want a change because I feel I have reached a saturation point here. They would be happy to be a referee from me, add I am applying for this post with their knowledge and consent.

I hope your company can better utilise my experience and qualifications. A copy of my resume, giving full details together with photocopies of certificates/testimonials are enclosed.

I look forward to hear from you soon.

With thanks,

306. Application for Accounts Clerk

Dear Sirs,

Having heard from one of my friends that you need an "Accounts Clerk" in your office, I offer my services for the post and hope that you will give me an opportunity of proving my worth to you.

The following are my qualifications which I hope you will find satisfactory.

Age : --
Education : --
Experience : --
Reference : --

Salary : --

It hardly needs mention here that I belong to a very respectable family.

I hope you will kindly give me an appointment for an interview. I assure you that I shall do my best to satisfy you in every way.

307. Application for a Manager's Post

Dear Sir,

I understand that you are in need of the services of an experienced Manager - "Just see if the following details will meet the requirements of your office!"

Qualifications :

   (i) --
   (ii) --
   (iii) --
   (iv) --

Experience :

   (i) --
   (ii) --

Special Knowledge :

   (i) --
   (ii) --
   (iii) --
   (iv) --

     Age : --

Present Salary and Other Benefits :

   (i) Pay Rs. -- per month
   (ii) Provident Fund contribution at the rate of -- with equal share from the employers.
   (iii) Average bonus has been 4 months basic pay (Rs. --)
   (iv) First Class to and for rail fare, once in year, for visiting native place Bhopal.

Minimum Expected Salary :

Rs. -- per month.

Notice Period :

3 months

Languages Known :

Foreign : English, -- and --

Indian : Hindi and Marathi

I shall be glad to discuss with you personally any further details you may require.

308. Employer's Letter to Cashier's Previous Employers for Reference

Dear Sir,

Mr. Vikas Bhalla has applied for the post of a cashier in our firm and has asked us to write to you for particulars as to his ability, honesty and general character. We shall be glad to have any information you can supply us regarding him and would like to know, if you found him competent enough to keep charge of accounts of a Travel Agency firm Naturally we wish to secure a man and who can be relied upon to work quickly and accurately and who is also thoroughly conversant with every details of a Travel Agency firm. Moreover, as large sums would have to pass through his hands, we should require to feel assured that he would be trustworthy in every respect, and of sober habits.

A very early reply is requested,

309. Reply to Above

Dear Sir,

In reply to your letter dated the 23rd September, we would like to inform you that Mr. Vikas Balla was in our employ for five years and he left us of his own accord as he wanted to go to his native place for some family affairs. We found him absolutely reliable. We are sorry to lose his services but wish him all success in life. We feel sure that you would never regret taking this young man into your employ.

310. Application for the Post of Engineer

Dear Sir,

I am writing in response to your advertisment in the March __ issue of the Hindustan Time for the post of production Engineer. As an experienced mechanical engineer with a desire to work in a dynamic work environment that offers unmatched opportunities through continuous training and career progression, I would like to be a part of your expanding multi-business company having links with technology leaders around the world.

After completing B Tech in mechanical Engineering from IIT, Mumbai, I did a specialised course in Auto CAD. Since 2003 I have been working as an production Engineer in Alfa-Laval, engaged in design and manufacture of dairy and distilleries plants and machinery. In this position, I am involved in designing the equipment for dairy and distillaries and have considerable knowledge of International codes and standards.

My resume enclosed with the application, provides additional information regarding any education, training experience, skills, achievements, and references. I would appreciate meeting with you to discuss how my experience could contribute to your prestigious company.

You can reach me at (022) - 17223745 between 8.00 a. m. and 6.00 p. m. or contact me via e-mail at rahul das@rediffmail.Com.

Sincerely

Rahul Das

Exclosure : 1) Resume 2) Copies of degrees and mark sheet and 3) Copy of experience certificate

311. Application to the Principal for the Issue of a Transfer Certificate

Dear Sir,

Respectfully I beg to say that my father has been transferred to Pune. There I have taken admission in Modern College. I have to deposit my T. C. there. I therefore request you to issue me my transfer certificate at the earliest and oblige.

Thanking you,

312. An Application to the Principal Requesting Him to Issue a Character Certificate

Dear Sir,

I was a student of your school from 2001 to 2005. I passed my Intermediate Examination in 2005. I am applying for a job in the State Bank of India. I have to submit a character certificate along with the application from. I, therefore, request you to issue me a character certificate and oblige.

313. An Application to the Principal for Full Fee Concession

Dear Sir,

Respectfully I beg to state that I am a student a class XI C. The financial condition of my father is not good. Thus I find it difficult to pay the college fees. I enjoyed full freeship in class X. I have always been a good student. Last year also I stood second in the Board Examination. Kindly grant me full concession in fee this year also. I shall be highly grateful to you for that.

314. An Application to the Principal Requesting Him to Grant Leave for Three Days

Dear Sir,

In my house some guests have arrived from Mumbai. My father is away from home on tour for some office work since Sunday. He will be back home after three days.

At home my mother is alone. There is nobody to help her except myself. Under the circumstances I request you to grant me leave of absence from school for three days from to-day.

Thanking you,

315. An Application to the Principal Requesting Him to Issue a Duplicate Copy of Marks-sheet

Dear Sir,

With due respect I beg to say that I have passed class XI as a regular student from your college. I was placed in first division. My Roll

No. was 114 - A. I have lost my original marks-sheet. I am in need of a duplicate copy of the same.

Kindly send a duplicate copy of my marks-sheet at the following address. A postal order for Rs. 5 is attached herewith.

316. Letter of Appointment

Dear Sir,

With further reference to you interview with our General Manager-Personnel, Mr. Kishor Sahani on October, 20--, we are pleased to appoint you an Sales Officer in our company. The terms and conditions of the offer, and offer details are enclosed in the from of company notes.

Please confirm, within 10 days of the receipt of this Letter of Appointment, your acceptance in writing, on the enclosed terms and conditions. You are required to join us as Sales Officer latest by -- December, 20--.

We wish you a successful and rewarding career with us.

317. Accepting the above Appointment

Dear Sir,

Thank you for your letter of Appointment dated -- November 20--, offering me the post of a Sales Officer in your so large and well-known establishment.

I am really glad to accept the post on the salary offered, and the terms and conditions attached with the appointment letter. I confirm the commencement of my work latest by -- December. However, I may join even earlier.

I want to assure you again, in no uncertain terms, that I would do my best to satisfy you and other superiors and colleagues, and to make a success of my job under you, in your company.

318. Testimonial

To whom it may concern

This is to certify that Mr. Ravindra Laxman Kale has been in our employ for over 3 years as a Stenographer, during which time we found his work and conduct beyond reproach. He is a sincere, accurate, hard-working and energetic stenographer. He can be entrusted with any confidential and important work related to his job.

He is leaving us in search of better employment, and we wish him all the best. We are sorry to dispense with his service because at present we have no promotional opportunity here for him.

319. Employer's Letter Seeking Reference

Dear Sir,

Mr. Devendra Laxman Naik who has been working with you as Assistant Accountant for the last 5 years, has applied for the post of Accountant in our company and has given the name of your firm as a reference.

We would like to know if his services with you in the capacity of an Asst. Accountant have been to your entire satisfaction, and if he is fully qualified, experienced and fit to shoulder the responsibility as Accountant in our establishment.

Further, we would very much appreciate any information you can give us regarding his conduct, sincerity, reliability and particularly his ability and skill to cope with the pressure of work as an Accountant.

We will treat all this information given to us as strictly confidential.

320. Favourable Reply to Above

Dear Sir,

I am glad to respond favourably to your reference enquiry concerning Mr. Devendra Laxman Naik dt -- July, 20--. He has been with us for the last 3 years, and has been working as Asstt. Accountant. He is really sincere, hard-working, and well-qualified. During his stay with us, we found his work and conduct most satisfying. We would certainly miss him but we are not in a position to promote him to the post of Accountant, as there is already a person in the position.

He is B. Com. (Hons). with advanced accountancy as a subject, and know his job well. Should you employ him as accountant in your firm, you may completely depend on him. He is reliable, trustworthy, and bears a good moral character.

He is going because you are offering him better prospects. We wish him all the success.

321. Letter of Resignation

Dear Sir,

Due to some personal reasons I am unable to continue my service in you firm. I, hereby, give a notice of thirty days to resign from my job of a Public Relations Officer. It is, therefore requested that I may please be relieved from my post of the expiry of the notice period.

Thanking you,

322. Character Certificate by a Gazetted Officer

To whom it may concern

This is to certify that Shri Rakesh Sohanlal Pande son of Shri Sohanlal Pande resident of C-1/2 Model Colony, Pune is personally known to me for the last two years.

He bears a good moral character.

I wish him success in his future career.

323. Letter of an Interview

Dear Sir,

With reference to your application dated -- August on the subject cited above, please present yourself for a personal interview before Regional Manager, at Hotel Hilton, Hyderabad on -- September at 2.30 p.m.

Please bring with you the original certificates and testimonials at the time of interview.

No travelling allowance will be payable for appearing for the interview.

324. Resignation from an Employee

Dear Sir,

For certain unavoidable circumstances in my family, it has become necessary for me to discontinue my present service. I, therefore, request that I may kindly be relieved of my present duties as soon as possible, in any case not later than the -- February, 2006.

My account in full may please be settled before that date.

Thanking you,

325. About Overcharged Statement

Dear Sir,

We are in receipt of your statement for March. But we are sorry to tell you that you statement has the following errors.

1. The special discount of 2% allowed on bulk purchases of Rs. -- and above has not been entered. Our total order was for Rs. -- worth of items.
2. The sum of Rs. -- for the return of empty packaging cases and bags has not been entered and adjusted.
3. Invoice No. -- for Rs. -- has been debited twice, once on February -- and again on March --.

Therefore, we request you to send us the amended bill for payment. As soon as we receive your revised and corrected bill, we shall be glad to send the cheque.

326. Request for Extension of Time to Repay Loan

Dear Mr. Patil,

You were good enough to grant me a lone of Rs. -- on -- August which becomes due for repayment next week-end. I was ready and prepared to make this repayment, but unfortunately, my father was involved in a very serious accident. Now he is in an intensive care unit of a local nursing home struggling for life.

I have to spend a lot on my father's hospitalisation, treatment and nursing. This sudden and unfortunate turn of events has made me quite unable to repay your loan immediately.

In these circumstances, I am to request you to extend the time of repayment of loan for a period of one month.

327. Releasing an Advertisement for Prime Land for a Resort

Dear Mr....

Subject : Advertisement for Availability of Prime Land for a Resort

We thank you for your letter of -- August 20-- together with a copy of your Advertisement tariff.

We are pleased to enclose an advertisement -- cms x -- cms to be inserted on the front page of your City Edition on Monday -- October 20 --

Also enclosed is a cheque No.... dated.... for Rs.... towards advance payment of the advertisement.

Thanks,

Yours Faithfully

--

Encl. 1. Cheque for Rs. --

2. Advertisement Matter

328. Requesting for Renewal of Lease

Dear Mr. Ramprakash

Regrading Renewal of Lease : -- Corporation Road

As you are aware our lease of the above office premises expires on -- April, 20-- as per the terms and conditions of the agreement. As we want to continue our business from this place, we request you to extend the lease for further period of -- years with effect from -- May 20 -- at the same terms and conditions.

In view of the high maintenance costs and increased rates of taxes on commercial property, we are willing to increase the present rent by --%. We hope this should satisfy you.

We look forward to an early reply so that a new lease agreement can be executed in time before the lapse of the present one.

329. For Subscription Renewal

Dear Reader,

We have been sending you regularly your most favorite magazine India Today and we are sure it has been of immense service to you and your family.

But to make sure you miss no issues, we would like to draw your attention to your Annual Subscription which will expire next month.

Will you please sign and return the enclosed form right now instructing us to renew your subscription.

And do keep in mind, the longer the term you specify, the more money you save.

330. Soliciting Advertising

Dear Sir,

We have the pleasure to offer our services to bring to your door a dumper crop of business by advertising for you in our monthly magazine which has become a craze for more that four lakhs and fifty thousand youths in the country, our circulation at present exceeding, -- copies.

In our March Issue, we wish to cover exciting articles on bikes. We are soliciting matching advertisements to catch up the attention of the youths.

The March Issue will present a most unusual and timely opportunity to publicise your very find products.

We shall, therefore, like to have your instructions in the matter.

A copy of the Advertisement Tariff is enclosed.

331. A Letter to the Municipal Commissioner Pointing Out the Need of a Public Park In Your Crowded City

Dear Sir,

Our small town is today facing many pressing problems. Among them the need for a public park has to be met with immediately.

The town is fast becoming overcrowded. Shops, business houses and residential buildings are coming up everywhere. But one of the most essential things needed is a fair-sized public park with properly equipped areas meant for children. Gardens are indeed, the lungs of a locality. It is such a place that provides relaxation, clean, healthy air and entertainment.

A public park in modern Pune is not an idle luxury. On the contrary, it is a vital necessity. Funds must be made available for it. After all, public health is at stake. May I expect you to proceed in this matter at your earliest?

332. A Letter to the Manager Requesting Permission to Visit a Factory

Dear Sir,

I am the General Secretary of the Student's Council of J. N. High School. Our school curriculum stresses that the students undertake projects and field work. We have a science laboratory and workshop where our students perform experiments and do a number of creative activities.

As a part of the training programme, our school has been arranging visits to various factories and mills from time to time.

I would like to bring a batch of twenty students to your factory if you could kindly grant us permission to do so. Each student will later be asked to submit a report on the visit.

We will be able to visit your factory on any day that is convenient to you.

We await your favourable reply.

333. Notifying Closing of a Branch

Dear Sir,

We regret to notify closure of our branch at Katraj dairy, Pune from January, 20-- on a account of transport difficulties.

All work relating to that branch will here after be undertaken by the head office at the above address.

334. Asking for Report on Creditability of a Firm

Dear Sirs,

We are having trouble collecting from M/s Raibahadur and Sons, Tadiwala Road, Pune. Their debts are long over-due and they have been avoiding payments.

We shall greatly appreciate, if you kindly oblige us by giving your impressions about the creditability of that firm.

We know, we are causing you much inconvenience. But we assure you that we shall not hesitate to reciprocate if we are entrusted with a similar task.

335. Introducing to Foreign Firms

Dear Sirs,

We have the pleasure to introduce ourselves as manufacturers and exporters of ready-made garments. We have been in the link for the last ten years, and it has been our proud privilege to have bagged very good orders from leading business houses abroad.

We participated in a big way in the ready-made garments. Fair held recently at Pragati Maidan, New Delhi and we have been fortunate enough to book business worth Rs. -- lakhs.

We have the advantage of having our own Designing, Weaving, Tailoring and Outfitting Departments under a panel of select technicians and experts whose workmanship has earned for us a unique distinction in colour design, fabric and finish, stitching and outfitting.

Besides the vast stock of varieties and novelties we have ready for you, we gladly undertake to get you what you order us for. Whereas we have served many foreign business houses, we earnestly wish to serve you too with our experience and specialisation.

We are sure, you will be greatly impressed with the samples which we shall send after hearing from you.

Assuring you of the best of our attention and co-operation.

336. Follow up Letter to a Foreign Firm

Dear Sir,

Sometime ago. Mr. Ravi Shah visited us, and we had the honour and privilege of showing him round our factory and various units of manufacturing, designing and outfitting.

He had selected a few samples which we had sent you last month.

We have, no doubt, in our minds, these samples would have met with your approval. We are anxious to know your requirements which will be supplied immediately on hearing from you.

We have, by now, brought out several other novelties which we are sure, will win your applause. We shall be glad to hear from you your additional demands which will also be made available, whenever you may desire.

Assuring you of the best of our attention.

337. Request for Releasing a Company from a Contract

Dear Sirs,

We regret to inform you that you have failed to maintain the supply of iron wire agreed upon in the above contract, with the result that production in our factory has declined. Accordingly, we have been forced to make supplementary arrangements at higher cost.

We have, therefore, most reluctantly decided to cancel the contract. We shall, however, be open to contract, when you are in a batter position to maintain supplies.

Enclosed please find a cheque in full and final settlement of the accounts.

338. Inviting a Representative of a Firm to Visit Factory

Dear Sirs,

We are glad to find the interest you have been good enough to show in our products. We have a vast variety of leather goods to offer, and we can undertake making goods of your choice. We earnestly feel, it will make things easy if you kindly arrange to detail your representative to visit us some day.

We shall take him round our factory to see for himself the novelties we have in store for you.

339. Informing of the Visit of a Representative

Dear Sirs,

We thank you for your letter of January --, 20--.

We have detailed our Sales Representative Mr. M. S. Patil to visit you next week.

He will discuss with you our requirements, and we hope you will supply the goods accordingly on the terms offered by you.

340. Booking a Stall in the Fair

Dear Sir,

Please book one stall in the name of New Age Fashion in the ensuing Garments Fair to be held at Pragati Maidan.

We are manufacturers and suppliers of ready-made garments to various countries of the world, and we are sure we shall be able to participate in a big way in the forthcoming fair.

341. Asking for Samples of Designs

Dear Sir,

We thank you for your visit to our Office on December --.

We are interested in a few designs of calendars and other publicity material. The designs should be sober and appealing but not provocative and exposed.

We shall appreciate if you can arrange to send us some samples next week.

342. Declining an Offer to Serve on the Committee

Dear Sir,

I thank you for your kind offer to me to serve on the Leather Manufacturers Consumers Committee.

I regret that as a result of my pre-occuptions I shall not be able to spare any time to be of some service to you.

I do, however, support the ideal before the committee.

343. A Letter to the Editor of a Newspaper Stressing the Need to Protect Trees from being Cut Down

Dear Sir,

Yesterday, a whole line of trees along University Road were cut down. This was a totally irresponsible action. We should not be so careless about our environment. Where was the need to cut down these trees? They provided shade, beauty and freshness to the area and promoted health by providing pure air. They made the environment clean. They also provided a haven for many endangered birds and animals. Now the entire area has already become hot, sultry and breezeless.

Where were the organisations like Friends Of Trees, Who always campaign for the protection of trees, when this heinous deed was being committed? Where were the other social welfare organisations who shout at the top of their voices for a clean Pune-Green Pune when this senseless deed was being carried out? Did the ones who gave such orders even think of the health and the cleanliness of the environment? It is authorities such as these who are to be held responsible for the total extinction of certain species of trees.

The organizations mentioned above should earnestly see to it that this kind of destruction, which has made many ardent treelovers sad, is not repeated. I earnestly suggest that the PMC undertake replanting of the trees in the locality as soon as possible.

344. Write a Letter to Advertising Agency/Newspaper for an Advertisement

Dear Sir,

Please arrange for three insertions on alternate days of the enclosed advertisement in the 'Lokmat' Pune, Nagpur and Mumbai edition. The insertions should be displayed, with design heading similar to the enclosed and large block capitals for the title, describing the nature of the vacancies.

REQUIRED ENGINEERS

A multidisciplinary company using mechanical, metallurgical, electrical and electronic engineering in its process and products and having integrated facilities like forging, casting, machning, tool room and others, requires engineers in the following department.

MACHINE SHOP : Graduate Engineers/Diploma Engineers in mechanical/production with about 2 years experience for a machine shop consisting of a battery of CNC lathes, capstans and Automats.

Send your detailed resume with present and expected CTC with in 10 days to

MAXEL ENGINEERS LTD.

PLOT NO. B/2, MIDC

HINGNA, NAGPUR.

We would like you to arrange for the same advertisement to be inserted for three alternate days in some popular newspapers of Vidarbha. Kindly recommend suitable dailies in which we could advertise our products and send us particulars of their charges for single and multiple insertions.

We will send you cheque for your charges on receipt of statement of account.

345. From an Author to Publisher for Accounts

Dear Sirs,

I regret to say that despite my repeated reminders and personal visits, you have not bothered to clear my accounts of royalty against the books, I have written for you.

You have been trying to put me off by dilatory tactics for the last three years. I have been bearing with you in my sincere wish not to spoil my relations with you. But there is a limit to patience.

I am afraid, if my accounts are not cleared within a fortnight, I shall seek redress through a court of law.

346. Reply to the Above

Dear Sir,

We are in receipt to your letter of January 10. We value our relations with our old authors. But we had some financial difficulties for some time.

We are thankful to you that you bore with us, and we assure you that we shall make at least a part-payment before the close of this month.

Assuring you of the best of our regards.

347. Regretting Delay in Payment

Dear Sirs,

We regret to have delayed clearing your account which was so unavoidable despite our sincere wish.

Enclosed please find a cheque of Rs. 2,000 on account which, we assure you,will be followed in two weeks time by another cheque in full settlement of the dues.

Please accept our apologies for failing to keep our accounts up-to-date.

We appreciate your courtesy in bearing with us.

348. Letter for Income-Tax Refund

Dear Sir,

Kindly refer to your Assessment Order dated July 20--. for the year, 20-- to -- in respect of our firm.

Since the amount deposited by us as Advance Income-Tax is in excess of the assessed, we are submitting a refund application form with the request that the balance amount may kindly be refunded at an early date.

349. Reply to Above

Dear Sir,

We are in receipt of your letter dated – July 20-- calling us on Jan. 10, 20-- for assessment.

I regret I shall be out on tour after Jan. 6, and I shall not be able to present myself in your office before the 1st week of Feb. 20--

It is therefore, requested that I may accordingly be given another date.

350. Asking for Contributions

Dear Sirs,

We are sure, you are fully aware of the activities of this society which has been rendering a great assistance to the needy and the poverty-stricken an also the victims of natural calamities.

Since our field of activity has greatly widened, we feel the need to enlarge our funds.

We would, therefore, greatly appreciate if you kindly remit us your generous donation for the cause of the suffering mankind.

□ □

E-mail

Introduction

Electronics communication, because of its speed and broad casting ability, is different from paper-based communication. Because the exchange of messages can be so fast, e-mail is more conversational that traditional letters.

As sending e-mail does not involve printing and copying, it is less expensive than any other channel of communication. E-mail allows complete flexibility during composing and drafting. While using e-mail, you may edit, revise, modify and redesign your message without printing and copying your message. You feel free to reshape your e-mail message before sending. Moreover, you have flexibility to receive or compose e-mail as per your convenience.

E-mail Address

Any computer running in a multiuser environment, each user has a unique user name or login name. The username combined with the computer's unique fully qualified domain name provides the user's unique E-mail address.

A complete E-mail address is made up of two parts - (1) The user name, (2) The host names It is like 1. user name @ 2. host name.

(1) User Name - The first part identifies the user's name to whom mail is to sent.

(2) Host Name - Second parts represent the fully qualified domain name of the server or host on which the user has an account.

These two parts is separated by an "@" symbol.

There are variants on E-mail address -

nstripathi@hotmail.com
diamondpublications@vsnl.net
rgopal-co@rediffmail.com
info@magnaprakashan.com

Advantages of E-mail

E-mail is fast replacing the telephone and the fax as the primary mode by communication. E-mail has a number of advantages over other modes of communications.

(1) Cost effective - E-mail is a cost effective communication medium. The cost communicating with others has nothing to do with the distance or the size of message.

(2) Time saving-very speedy - E-mail is instantaneous your message can reach the other end of the globe in a seconds. It is different that your recipient may not be present to receive your message at the same time.

(3) No wastage of papers - E-mail has tremendously reduce the use of papers in the offices.

(4) Not disturbing - Unlike the telephone or the fax, it does not ring in between an important meeting or in the midnight. E-mail can be checked and replied at one's convenience. It does not have to be replied to at the very moment, unlike the phone.

E-mail Account

Before using the E-mail, facility, you have to open an E-mail account with a password. Account can be open with the ISP (internet service providers) which is a paid account, while lot of websites today provides this facility free of cost.

Some popular free web based services are :

(1) http://mail.yahoo. com

(2) http://mail.sify. com

(3) http://www.hotmail.com

(4) http://www.rediffmail.com

(5) http://mail.indya.com

You log on to any of these sites and then register your-self as a new user.

Formatting E-mail Messages

Although e-mail systems normally provide you with a ready-made format, you need to follow standard writing conventions and use the existing format effectively. Thus, formatting e-mail messages demands awareness of current e-mail conventions and standard practices. In order to write an appropriate e-mail, you should format your e-mail correctly.

When you receive an Internet e-mail message, it usually contains many lines before the beginning of the actual text. These lines consist of the "header" of the message. Most of it is a record of the path the message took from the sender's computer to your computer. Headers also often contain a time and date stamp and an indication of whether files are attached to the message.

The three most important pieces of information in the header are the e-mail addresses of the sender and the recipient, and a subject line that tells what the message is about. All e-mail messages contain these three pieces of information.

When you send an e-mail message, your program usually inserts your name, return e-mail address and date automatically. Therefore, you need not type your name, e-mail address and date again. You just need to fill in the "To" line with the recipient's e-mail address, the "Subject" line with a clear and concise description of the subject of your message, the CC line with the e-mail address of anyone who is to receive a copy of your e-mail message, and BCC line with the e-mail address of anyone who is to receive a blind copy of your e-mail message.

E-mail includes the following :
- O Heading
- O Salutation
- O Body
- O Closing
- O Signature

(1) Heading :

The heading segment of an e-mail includes the following six elements :

(1) DATE

(2) FROM

(3) TO

(4) SUBJECT

(5) CC

(6) BCC

Date : The Dateline indicates the date on which the e-mail was written. It includes the day, month, year and the exact time. When you send an e-mail message, the date line usually appears automatically.

From : The From line contains the sender's name and e-mail address. The name does not include any personal title such as Ms., Mrs., or Dr. When you send an e-mail message, your return address usually appears automatically.

To : The To line includes the recipient's e-mail address.

Subject : The Subject line summarises the topic of the e-mail in a few words. It includes clear and complete information about the theme of the e-mail in a phrase form.

Examples :

SUBJECT : ITC Annual Conference 2006

SUBJECT : TACON 2005 Proposal

SUBJECT : Confirmation of participation in NBT seminar on editing

CC : The CC line (carbon copy) may include the e-mail address of anyone who is to receive a copy of your e-mail message. It is an optional line.

BCC : The BCC line (blind carbon copy) may include the e-mail address of anyone who is to receive a blind copy of your e-mail message. It is an optional line.

(2) Salutation :

If you use e-mail as a means to reach out to people outside your organisation. Use the same name as in the To line. You may add a personal title such as Ms., Mrs., Mr., or Dr. However, you may omit a salutation if you use e-mail to send information inside your organisation.

(3) Body :

The body of an e-mail contains the message or the main content of the e-mail. You may organise the content in your e-mail carefully. In the first paragraph, consider a friendly opening and then a statement of the main point. The next paragraph should begin justifying the importance of the main point. In the next few paragraphs, continue this justification with background information and supporting detail. The closing paragraph should restate the purpose of the e-mail and, in some cases, request some type of action.

(4) Closing :

You may conclude an external e-mail message with an appropriate closing such as Best regards, Kind regards, Regards, Sincerely, Yours faithfully, Thank you and regards, All the best, etc. Capitalise the first word only.

(5) Signature :

The signature line in an e-mail message generally contains only the writer's name. However, it may sometimes include the title and organisation of the sender.

Standard E-mail Practices

You need to follow standard e-mail practices and learn e-mail etiquette or netiquette to write effective e-mail messages. The following suggestions will help you to organise and present your e-mail messages systematically.

(1) Check Your Mailbox Daily

As speed is the main advantage of using e-mail, everyone wants to get quick response to his/her e-mail. Check your mailbox daily so that you can read every e-mail message sent to you and respond swiftly. In case, you cannot response because you do not have enough information, send an e-mail acknowledgement.

(2) Be Correct

Many people tend to be casual while sending an e-mail message. You should take special care about accuracy, which includes both, i. e., accuracy of information as well as accuracy of presentation. It is very important that you assure yourself of the accuracy of information before you click the send button. Double-check the following :

- the electronic address/addresses of the receiver;
- the subject line,
- basic content of the e-mail message; and
- the attachments.

Also, you need to review, edit and revise your e-mail message in order to improve the quality of its presentation. Review your e-mail message to analyse whether your message can achieve its purpose. Edit it to correct its format, mechanics, grammar, spelling and punctuation. You may use spelling and grammar check.

(3) Be Brief

You may use e-mail effectively to convey non-sensitive simple messages. E-mail may not be very suitable for conveying complex or non-sensitive information. So, keep your e-mail message short. No one likes to read very lengthy e-mail messages. Avoid unnecessary information, wordy expressions, repetitions, and exaggeration. Ensure that your e-mail message makes its point in the fewest words possible. Keep your sentences and paragraphs short.

(4) Be Formal

E-mail is a formal channel of communication and you should use formal language. Use standard writing techniques and follow professional writing conventions. Use standard English and do not get too informal even if you know the receiver very closely. Avoid using emotional expressions, informal words, personal remarks, humorous statements, jokes, etc. Keep the purpose in mind, and resist distraction.

(5) Maintain Readability

In order to make your message easy to read, keep your computer screen in mind when you compose your e-mail message. Use design elements such as introductory summary, headings, side-headings, listings, etc. in order to improve readability of longer e-mail messages.

(6) Care About Tone

Avoid using a tactless or negative tone that can lead to confusion and misunderstanding. Use a formal but conversational tone which gives a personal touch to your e-mail. Adapt your expression to the demands of the situation and the needs of your readers. You may use first person pronouns (i. e., I, we) and conversational contractions (you'll, he'll, she'll, can't, don't, doesn't, etc.)

E-mail Format

Mail	Addresses	Calender	Notepad	anindya@rediffmail.com (Sign Out)		
Check Mail	Compose			Search Mail Mail Options		
Check Other Mail	Previous	Next	Back of Messages		Printable View-Full	
Edit	Delete	Reply	Reply All	Forward	as attachment	Move to folder
Folder [Add]	DATE :					
Inbox	FROM :					
Draft	TO : .... SUBJECT :					
Sent	CC :					
Bulk (Empty)	BCC : .... Dear Mr. Pranav,					
Trash (Empty)	....					
My Folders (Hide)						
	Thank you and regards, Aniket Desai Manager (HR)					

Emoticons

At the time of sending E-mail to your friend or else, you fell to express your emotions, but your recipient can't see or hear you.

However people have make it easy this by developing special symbols or EMOTICONS. It is called smiley too. Emoticons or smiley are to express your basic emotions and also act as a short hand.

Example :

Emoticon	What it means	-	-
:)	a smile, happy	:-)	a smile with nose
;)	a wink	:(	a frown
>:-C	someone mad or annoyed	:->	devious smile
:-0	shouting	<-1	grim
:-D	laughing	:-0	shouting loudly
X-(	dead	:-P	sticking out tongue
O:-)	an angle	:-C	crying
<g>	grin	@>-,-'-	a rose
		1-1	a sleep
		: ??	determined
		: ??	not happy
		: ??	wow
		):-)	mischievous
		:-x	shocked
		:-Ozz	bored
		|-O	snoring
		:-v	talking
		:*)	only joking
		:-Q	confused
		:-S	lost for words
		|:-)	imaginative

Acronyms

Acronyms or abbreviation are used in E-mail, chat, and new group as a online short hand. These can be used in all upper case (capital letters) or all lower case (small letters).

Acronyms or Abbreviation for E-mail

Acronyms		Meaning
AFK	-	Away from Keyboard
ASL	-	Age / sex / location
AAMOF	-	as a matter of fact
BAK	-	Bank at keyboard
BBIAF	-	Be back in a flash
BBL	-	Be back later
BRB	-	Be right back
BBS	-	Bulletin board system
BTW	-	By the way
CU	-	See you
CUL	-	See you later
DL	-	Download
FTF or F2F	-	Face to Face
FAQ	-	Frequently asked question
FYI	-	For your information
GMTA	-	Great mind think a like
IC	-	In character (playing a role)
HTH	-	Hope this helps
HHOJ	-	Ha, ha, only joking
HHOS	-	Ha, ha, only serious
IAC	-	In any case
IAE	-	In any event
IM	-	Instant message
IMO	-	In my opinion
IOW	-	In other word
JK	-	Just kidding
LOL	-	Laughing out loud
LTR	-	Later
LTNS	-	Long time no see
LTNT	-	Long time no type
NP	-	No problem
OOC	-	Out of character
RP	-	Role play
RL	-	Real life
O/C	-	Oh, I see

T/A	-	Thanks in advance
WB	-	Welcome back
WTG	-	Way to go
:D	-	A smile

SMS Dictionary

ABT	-	about
ADN	-	any day now
AFAIK	-	as far as I know
AKA	-	also known as
ASAP	-	as soon as possible
ATB	-	all the best
B4	-	before
B4N	-	bye for now
BBS	-	be back soon
BFN	-	bye for now
CWOT	-	complete waste of time
CWYL	-	chat with you later
DTRT	-	do the right thing
DYK	-	do you know
EOD	-	end of discussion
FOAF	-	Friend of a friend
FOC	-	free of charge
FWIW	-	for what it's worth
FYEO	-	for your eyes only
G and BIT	-	grin and bear it
G2G	-	got to go
GAL	-	get a life
GBH	-	great big hug
GOK	-	god only knows
GOWI	-	get on with it
GR8	-	great
HAG1	-	have a good one
HIH	-	hope it helps
HSIK	-	how should I know
HAND	-	have a nice day
IC	-	I see

IGTP	-	I get the point
IJWTK	-	I just want to know
IMO	-	in my opinion
INPO	-	in no particular order
IUSS	-	if you say so
JAM	-	just a minute
JIC	-	just in case
JK	-	just kidding
JTLYK	-	just to let you know
KHYF	-	know how you feel
KIT	-	keep in touch
KUTGW	-	keep up the good work
LL and P	-	live long and prosper
NOYB	-	none of your business
NE	-	any
NE1	-	any one
OBTW	-	oh! by the way
OMG	-	oh! my God
OTOH	-	on the other hand
PCM	-	please call me
PPL	-	People
PRT	-	party
RUOK?	-	are you o.k.?
SMEi	-	someone
THX	-	Thanks
TMI	-	too much information
TOY	-	thinking of you
TXTIN	-	texting
URT1	-	you are the one
VBS	-	very big smile
W8AM	-	wait a minute
WB	-	welcome back
WYSIWYG	-	what you see is what you get
WAN2	-	want to
WUWH	-	wish you were here
XLNT	-	Excellent
YBS	-	you will be sorry

Commercial Abbreviations

@	-	at the rate of
a/c	-	account
A. D.	-	Acknowledgement due
ad val	-	according to value
advt.	-	advertisment
A. M.	-	Ante Meridiem (before noon)
amt.	-	amount
a/o	-	account of
A/S	-	Account Sales
AGM	-	Annual General Meeting
ATM	-	Automated Teller Machine
attn.	-	for the attention of
ATV	-	All-terrain vehicle
approx.	-	approximately
B. C.	-	Before Christ
B/E	-	Bill of Exchange
b. f.	-	brought forward
B/L	-	Bill of Landing
BP	-	Bills payable
B/R	-	Bills Receivable
B.S.	-	Bill of Sale
b.s	-	balance sheet
B2B	-	Business-to-Business
C.A	-	Chartered Accountant
CC	-	Carbon Copy
c.i.f.	-	cost, insurance and freight
Co.	-	Company
c/o	-	care of
C.O.D.	-	Cash on delivery
Co.op.	-	Co-operative
C/R	-	Company's Risk
CD	-	Compact Disc
CAD	-	Computer - aided design
CCTV	-	Closed - circuit television
CD-I	-	compact disc interactive
CD-R	-	compact disc recordable

CD-Rom	-	compact disc read-only-memory
CD-RW	-	Compact disc Rewritable
CPI	-	Consumer Price Index
CV	-	Curriculum Vitae
D.O.B.	-	Date of Birth
D.A.	-	Dearness Allowance
DTP	-	Desktop Publishing
DVD	-	Digital Videodisc
d/a	-	documents against acceptance
D/n	-	Debit note
Do.	-	ditto (the same)
D/o	-	delivery order
doz	-	dozen
d/p	-	documents against payment
Dr	-	Debtor/Doctor
dpt.	-	Department
esp.	-	especially
e.g.	-	for example
encl.	-	enclosed
ext.	-	extension
Etc.	-	Etcetera; and so forth
ed.	-	edition
ed.	-	editor
et. seq.	-	and the following
ex.	-	ex godown (from godown)
ex.	-	example
exc.	-	exchange
E. and O. E.	-	errors and omissions excepted
fig.	-	figure
F.O.B.	-	Free on Board
F.O.R.	-	Free on Rail
Fao.	-	For the attention of
Ft.	-	feet, foot
gn.	-	general
gr. wt.	-	gross weight
GHQ	-	general headquarters
govt.	-	government

G.M.T.	-	Greenwich Mean Time
GPO	-	General Post Office
Hon.	-	Honourable
hr.	-	hour
ht.	-	height
HE	-	His Excellency
HGV	-	heavy goods vehicle
HR	-	Human Resource
HTML	-	Hypertext mark-up Language
HTTP	-	Hyper Text Transfer Protocol
i. c.	-	in charge
i. e.	-	that is
imp.	-	important
inc.	-	incorporated
inc.	-	including
inf.	-	infra (below)
inv.	-	invoice
I.O.U.	-	I owe you
ital.	-	italics
ID	-	Identification
IQ	-	Intelligence quotient
ISBN	-	International Standard Book Number
ISDN	-	Integrated Service Digital Network
ISP	-	Internet service provider
IT	-	Information Technology
Ibid	-	in the same place
I.S.D.	-	International Subscriber Dialing
Jr.	-	Junior
K.	-	Kilo
K.g.	-	Kilogram
Km.	-	Kilometer
Kw.	-	Killowatts
Kph.	-	Kilometers per hour
L/c	-	Letter of credit
Ltd.	-	Limited
LL.B.	-	Bachelor of Laws
LAN	-	Local Area Network

M.	-	Minute
Max.	-	Maximum
Mfg.	-	Manufacturing
m.g.	-	milligram
misc.	-	Miscellaneous
m.m.	-	Millimeter
M.B.B.S.	-	Bachelor of Medicine and Bachelor of Surgery
M.D.	-	Doctor of Medicine, Managing Director
M.L.A.	-	Member of Legislative Assembly
MOD	-	Ministry of Defence
MOT	-	Ministry of Transport
MP	-	Member of Parliament
MPV	-	Multi Purpose Vehicle
Ms	-	Manuscript
MSc, M.Sc.	-	Master of Science
Mth.	-	Month
Mgr.	-	Manager
Mtge	-	Mortgage
N.B.	-	Note bene (mark well) (Note well)
No.	-	Number
o.c.	-	office copy
o.d.	-	on demand
o.s.	-	out of stock
p.a.	-	per annum
pc.	-	Per Cent
pd.	-	Paid
pkg.	-	Packing
p.m.	-	Per month
P.N.	-	Promissory Note
P.O.	-	Postal Order
Pro.	-	for
Pro. tem.	-	For the time being
Prox.	-	Proximo, next month
P.S.	-	Postscript
P.T.O.	-	Please Turn Over
P.M.	-	Post Meridiem (Afternoon)
Ph.D.	-	Doctor of Philosopy

pc.	-	Personal Computer
PDF	-	Protable Document Format
PIN	-	Personal Indentification Number
PR	-	Public Relations
PP.	-	Pages
RAM	-	Random Access Memory
Rd.	-	Road
ref.	-	refer, reference
reg.	-	registration
ROM	-	Read only memory
RPI	-	Retail Price Index
RRP	-	Recommended Retail Price
RSVP	-	Please reply
RTF	-	Rich Text Format
Re.	-	Refer or referring to
reg.d	-	registered
retd.	-	returned, retired
R.P.	-	Reply Paid
Sec.	-	Secretary
Senr.	-	Senior
sr.	-	Senior
STD	-	Subscriber Trunk Dialing
St	-	Street
tr.	-	tare (weight)
TM	-	Trademark
TOEFL	-	Test of English as Foreign Language
UGC	-	University Grant Commission
UFO	-	Unidentified Flying Object
viz	-	Namely
WAN	-	Wide Area Network
WAP	-	Wireless Application Protocol
wt.	-	weight
WWW	-	World wide web

☐ ☐